"Why is everyone being so nice? What do they want?"

"They're nice people. No one expects anything from you." The light in Doug's brain popped on. His assessment of Tabitha made him both sad and angry. The word that described her—*used*.

She shook her head. "No. People always have an agenda."

"Not this time." He held the door open for her.

"I wish I could believe that."

"Give it time. We'll convince you that we genuinely care about you and want to help."

Her jaw dropped. "You don't even know me."

"But we want to." Doug continued down the path to his SUV. He glanced over his shoulder and found Tabitha staring at him. "Are you coming?"

"Fine."

Confident she'd follow, Doug held up his key fob and hit the start button.

The SUV exploded. The blast threw him backward into a parked car.

Flames shot from the SUV, warming his skin. His ears rang, and his head whirled. Debris floated in the air, and a dark haze drifted above him.

Had Tabitha survived?

Award-winning, bestselling author **Sami A. Abrams** grew up hating to read. It wasn't until her thirties that she found authors who captured her attention. Most evenings, you can find her engrossed in a romantic suspense novel. She lives in Northern California but will always be a Kansas girl at heart. She has a love of sports, family and travel. However, writing her next story in a cabin at Lake Tahoe tops her list.

Books by Sami A. Abrams

Love Inspired Suspense

Deputies of Anderson County

Buried Cold Case Secrets
Twin Murder Mix-Up
Detecting Secrets
Killer Christmas Evidence
Witness Escape

Visit the Author Profile page at LoveInspired.com.

Witness Escape

SAMI A. ABRAMS

LOVE INSPIRED SUSPENSE
INSPIRATIONAL ROMANCE

LOVE INSPIRED® SUSPENSE
INSPIRATIONAL ROMANCE

ISBN-13: 978-1-335-63823-6

Witness Escape

Love Inspired
22 Adelaide St. West, 41st Floor
Toronto, Ontario M5H 4E3, Canada
www.LoveInspired.com

Printed in Lithuania

Recycling programs for this product may not exist in your area.

MIX
Paper | Supporting responsible forestry
FSC® C021394

There hath no temptation taken you but such as is common to man: but God is faithful, who will not suffer you to be tempted above that ye are able; but will with the temptation also make a way to escape, that ye may be able to bear it.

—*1 Corinthians* 10:13

This book is dedicated to my friend Brenda Schulte.
She is my cheerleader and the voice of encouragement
when I'm discouraged with my writing.
Love you, Brenda Sue!

ONE

Wednesday, 7:00 p.m.

The warm day working with Valley Spring Fire Department Captain Phillip Scott on the recent arson case had sapped Detective Doug Olsen's energy. Or maybe it had more to do with the disappearance and probable death of his Army buddy and good friend, DEA agent Michael Lane. A man who'd stood by him and vowed to help find evidence to put the person responsible for murdering Doug's wife behind bars. Either way, Doug had hit his limits for the day.

He plodded toward a booth at the back of the local diner, Main Street Eats. He'd discarded his Kevlar vest, but sweat continued to drip between his shoulder blades. The evening temperatures had hung on, and he relished the cool interior of the restaurant.

The new owners had renovated the place into a fifties throwback café, and the customers loved the new vibe. Most days, he appreciated the atmosphere, but today wasn't one of those days. A cool drink—or two—plus dinner called to him.

The greasy food aroma from the grill made his stomach growl. He hadn't eaten since breakfast, which consisted of a quick bowl of cereal. Not something that would stay with a person for twelve hours. The sun hung low on the horizon and inched toward disappearing until tomorrow. He needed food, rest, and answers. Not necessarily in that order, but he'd take the meal first.

"Evening, Detective Olsen." Carl, one of the locals, greeted him. The man wore his typical Vietnam Veteran's cap. The two had shared war stories many times over the past few years. Different wars, different challenges. Vietnam and Afghanistan, but he and Carl understood each other's experiences on a basic level.

"Hey, Carl." Tinged with guilt but not wanting to get roped into a verbal exchange, he waved at the older gentleman and continued toward the back booth.

Several patrons greeted him along the way. He smiled and returned the gesture. He hated dismissing Carl and the others, but if he stopped, a conversation would ensue. And right now, he desperately craved alone time with his thoughts.

The black plastic squeaked beneath him as he slid onto the bench seat. He placed two cell phones on the red retro table and sighed. His shoulders sagged. Doug had prayed for the past five years that he'd find enough evidence to convict businessman and drug dealer Tommy Wade for murdering his wife, Christine. So maybe Tommy hadn't pulled the trigger, but he'd ordered the hit. Doug knew it. The police department in his hometown of Westmount, Indiana, knew it. The DEA knew it. Most likely, the FBI, ATF, and all the other alphabet-soup agencies knew it. But no one could put the proverbial smoking gun in Tommy's hands. And even if they could, evidence had a habit of disappearing or having holes in it like Swiss cheese by the time the district attorney reviewed it.

Six months ago, Doug started working behind the scenes with his friend to bring down Wade's entire operation. The drugs flowing through Anderson County made him sick, as did Wade's untouchable status. But his hope deflated when Michael went missing and was presumed dead. The eyewitness saw Michael on the boat moments before it exploded. And his body hadn't been found. The evidence left little hope that his friend had survived. There was no doubt in Doug's mind the responsibility for yet another person's demise landed at Tommy's feet.

Doug had retrieved Michael's special burner phone and a few files from his friend's apartment earlier that day, hoping to find anything that would help him continue the investigation into the drug dealer slash murderer. Michael had hinted he was on to something big, but Doug had no idea what. They hadn't had an opportunity to discuss his friend's latest findings.

"Here's your coffee, Detective." The diner's new waitress Beth Smith placed a mug in front of him. "Would you like a menu, or are you ready to order?"

He lifted his gaze to the petite brunette with the most intriguing green eyes. The woman stood beside him poised with a pen and pad of paper. She looked familiar, but he had no idea from where. Too tired to think straight, he set aside the mental puzzle for another day. He waved off the menu. No need to peruse the items. He had them memorized. Besides, tonight was all about comfort food. "Cheeseburger and fries, please."

"Sure thing." Funny how the woman rarely made eye contact with anyone. She reminded him of a scolded puppy, and that gave him pause.

"Thanks, Beth."

She nodded and hurried to the kitchen.

Thankful Beth had remembered his standing drink order, he sipped the dark brew and closed his eyes. Life had taken yet another turn. *Why, God? I want to honor my wife and put Wade behind bars.* Christine deserved better than her killer going free. Too many years had passed without justice. And the guilt of not protecting her continued to plague him.

The bell above the door rang, pulling him from his thoughts. He glanced at Beth, who stood staring wide-eyed at the entrance. A family of four strolled in and sat near the front of the diner. After a moment, she relaxed—if you could call it that. She bustled over and greeted the two adults and their young children. She placed coloring page menus in front of the youngsters, then extracted two small crayon boxes that held three crayons each and handed each child a set.

On her way to the counter, she scanned the room again. Her gaze lingered on the front window with a view of Main Street. Dusk had fallen, and the glow from the streetlight threw shadows along the edges of the sidewalk. Something about her actions sent his detective senses on high alert.

The owners of Main Street Eats spoke highly of Beth, and Doug had never had any reason to question her presence in the diner since she started working there, but the fear in her movements concerned him. Almost as if someone had abused her.

Since he'd left the Army and started working for the Anderson County Sheriff's Department, he'd seen his fair share of domestic violence cases. It baffled him how people treated each other that way. He'd give almost anything to have

Christine back, and meanwhile there were men and women who abused the ones they claimed to love.

He made a mental note to keep an eye on the new waitress in case his instincts had hit the target. Maybe he'd do a little digging to ensure no one had harmed the woman and it was only his imagination running wild.

He returned his attention to Michael's cell phone and punched in his friend's passcode. Thankfully, Michael was predictable and used the same two passwords for all his devices and accounts. Doug had lectured him about security on multiple occasions, but Michael held his ground. One password, his favorite baseball team—Guardians. The other, the date they changed the team's name, 72321. Right now, he wanted to hug the man for not listening.

Doug scrolled through his friend's contacts, consisting of three people. Doug, Michael's boss, and the initials TW. TW? He scratched his jaw. Michael said he had an informant. Maybe that's who the initials belonged to.

He opened the text messages between Michael and the TW person and read.

Michael: You can do it. I know you can.

TW: I'm scared. What if something goes wrong?

Michael: I'll hide you until it's over.

TW: Promise?

Michael: Yes.

TW: Okay. I'll do it.

Michael: Thank you, Tabitha.

Doug sat up straight. TW's a woman? Who was Tabitha, and where had Michael hidden her? Doug's number one priority became finding this woman—for her sake and his. If the text referred to Tommy Wade like he suspected, he refused to let the slimebag destroy another life. With Michael missing and probably dead, the woman needed help.

Beth approached and placed his plate on the table. "Here you go, Detective."

"Looks good. Thank you." He smiled at her and unrolled his silverware from the napkin.

The door chimed again, and Beth jolted.

A small group of teens chattered as they strolled to a table and sat.

Doug's brow furrowed. The woman's eyes widened, and her chest rose and fell at a rapid rate.

She turned to go.

"Beth, wait." He reached out but her jumpiness made him withdraw his hand before making contact.

"Is there something else I can get for you?" She fisted the hem of her apron.

"No, it's not that. It's just…" He exhaled. "Are you okay?"

"I'm fine," she squeaked.

"If you're sure."

She bobbed her head up and down.

Doug pulled a business card from his wallet and jotted down his personal cell phone number. "I'd like you to take this and call me if you ever need anything."

"I don't need—"

He held up his palm. "Please, it'll make me feel better." He debated whether he should talk with her boss. Something was seriously off.

Beth took the card from his fingers and tucked it in the back pocket of her black jeans. "Thank you." Her voice so soft he had a hard time hearing her words.

He watched her walk away and wondered if he'd done the right thing by not pressing harder.

The smell of greasy fries and grilled beef made his stomach growl. He dug into the burger, enjoying the solitary moment, but his eyes never wavered from the timid waitress. He chuckled at himself. Stalker much? But he couldn't deny that the woman's apparent anxiety troubled him.

A protector by nature, Doug wanted to reach out and convince her to confide in him. He'd struggled for years with guilt over his wife's death, but God had helped him through those times. One of the lessons life had taught him was that he couldn't save everyone. And he'd embraced that truth—mostly. Despite that bit of wisdom, something about Beth made him want to try to save her.

The door chimed again, and a man in a tailored suit strolled in. He studied the patrons in the restaurant with laser-like precision.

Doug's gaze shifted to Beth.

She spun and hurried into the kitchen like the building had caught fire.

The man continued his scan of the diner as if looking for someone specific, then turned and walked out.

Uncertain of what he'd just witnessed, but sure of one thing—trouble had found Beth, and she needed his help whether she asked for it or not.

Tabitha Wilson's worst nightmare had caught up with her. Her breaths came in short pants as she smacked the crash bar of the diner's kitchen door. She hurried into the darkening alleyway that connected with the small staff parking lot. She plastered herself against the brick wall and tipped her head back against the hard surface. Tears burned behind her eyes.

How had Clark Bretton, Tommy Wade's second-in-command, found her?

Michael had promised to keep her safe. Where was he? He hadn't answered his phone in twenty-four hours. She was worried about him…about her hidden identity. The man had checked in with her twice a day over the past couple of weeks—until yesterday.

She pushed off the wall and raced toward her car in the employee parking lot. She had to leave before Clark discovered her—assuming he hadn't already. Two weeks of peace—gone.

A flat rear tire on her vehicle sent a jolt of panic through her. She skidded to an abrupt halt. Her stomach threatened to revolt. She had to get away from Clark. If the man grabbed her, she was a dead woman.

Instead of handing the task off to one of his minions, Tommy might kill her himself for running away. But if he knew about the murder evidence against him that she'd given to Agent Lane, not to mention the accounting data she'd collected as a backup for her own peace of mind, she could kiss a quick death goodbye. She shuddered at the images burned into her brain from the video she'd risked her life to acquire for Agent Lane. The one of Tommy torturing a man for disobedience.

How had she been so stupid to get involved with Tommy?

Trees towered beyond the pavement, casting shadows across the parking lot amplifying her unease. Tears streamed down her cheeks. "Michael, where are you?" she whispered into the night.

"Beth?" A deep baritone voice sent shivers up her neck and over her scalp.

She spun and came face-to-face with Detective Olsen. Knees trembling, she placed her hand on the trunk of the car to steady herself. "Detective. It's only you."

"Doug. Please. And yes, it's me." The streetlight illuminated his worried expression. "Can I help you with anything?"

A refusal sat on the tip of her tongue, then she thought better of turning down his offer. "I... um...could use some help changing my tire."

He glanced at the offending circle of rubber and scratched his jaw. His fingernails scaped against his five o'clock shadow. "Why don't I drop you off at home after your shift, and you can come back tomorrow during the daylight to retrieve your vehicle?"

Tabitha pinched the bridge of her nose. She'd just walked out on her job. How would she explain it to her boss? "No. That's okay. I can do it."

"I'm not saying I won't. I'd hoped to get it repaired for you in the morning."

She tilted her head back and peered up at the

man. His brown hair, not quite a military hair-cut, but short and neat. His brown eyes held a sincerity about them, but she couldn't trust her judgment. Why the generosity? What did he want from her? "Just the tire, please. I appreciate your kindness, but I'd prefer to keep my car with me."

He opened his mouth, then closed it. "The tire it is. Do you have your keys?"

Tabitha nodded and pulled them from her jeans pocket. Michael had drummed into her brain the importance of keeping her keys with her at all times.

"Go ahead and pop the trunk. I'll get the spare on and get you on your way."

"Thanks, Doug." She hit the unlock button on her key fob. The trunk bounced open. Her gaze darted along the tree line and across the darkened lot. Maybe Clark hadn't seen her, and her new identity remained intact. Then again, when had life ever been kind to her? She chuffed. *Never.*

"I hate to be that person, but you ran out of Main Street Eats rather fast. If you need to go back to work or clock out and get your things, that's okay by me. I'll get the tire all fixed up while you do what you need to." He jutted his chin toward the building.

She glanced down at her apron. Doug had a point. She had to return to the diner and apologize for her abrupt departure. "I think that might be a good idea." Tabitha pocketed her keys. Call her paranoid, but Michael was right. Having a way to escape gave her a sense of security.

Doug dropped the spare tire on the ground then grabbed the jack from the compartment under the trunk floor. "Would you like me to walk you back?"

Tabitha's heart rate kicked up a notch. No. She refused to allow her anxiety to take over. She'd made it this far, and determination fueled her to finish what she'd started. If Clark had seen her, he'd have grabbed her by now. Most likely, the man had moved on—for the moment. Then again, what if he hadn't? A shiver rippled through her.

"Beth?"

She blinked. The change of names still threw her at times. At least Beth had similarities to Tabitha. Michael had chosen it for that very reason.

"No, I can do it." Her gaze drifted to the alleyway that led to the rear door. The path seemed to stretch forever. She drew in a deep breath and plodded to the diner.

Hand on the door handle, she whipped her gaze from side to side. The safety she'd enjoyed for the last couple of weeks had disappeared. Clark had zeroed in on her location. It was only a matter of time until he found her and dragged her back to Tommy.

She blew out a breath and entered the diner. After apologizing to her boss, who told her they had it covered and to go home, she collected her tips, hung her apron on a hook, and returned to the lot.

A working tire on her car greeted her. "That was fast. Thank you for changing it."

Doug shut the trunk, brushed his hands together, and placed his fists on his hips. "Glad I could help." He pivoted to face her. His brown eyes locked onto her. "Is there anything else I can do for you?"

Her breath caught. It was as if the man saw right through her. And she didn't like it. She shook her head. "Thank you, but I'm going to head home." Tabitha scooted past him and slipped into the driver's seat.

"Call me if you need me." Doug gave a slight wave and stepped aside.

Pulling away from Main Street, she released a long breath. Her gaze bounced back and forth from the rearview mirror to the road ahead. The quiet neighborhoods stretched ahead. No headlights followed. She debated her next move. Stay in Valley Springs, Indiana, or find another location to hide?

Minutes from her rental house, Tabitha hit the

speed dial for Michael, desperate to talk with him. Tonight had rattled her. "Come on, pick up. I don't know what to do." She hated depending on him, but the man had shown her nothing but kindness.

"Hello?"

She heard the hum of an engine in the background. "Where have you been?"

The male voice on the other end paused for a long moment. "Beth?"

Her heart rate sped up, and a whimper threatened to escape. Why did Doug have Michael's phone? And what happened to Michael?

"Beth, is that you?"

How should she answer that? Her mind spun, but few options presented themselves. "Yes." She sniffed and turned onto her street. "Why do you have that phone?"

"It's my friend's."

Neither she nor Doug appeared willing to say Michael's name. And she sure wasn't going to out the man trying to save her life. She pulled into her driveway and shifted the car into Park. Without disconnecting, she scooped up her phone and exited the vehicle. What should she do? It wasn't like she could ignore Doug.

"Beth, tell me what's going on."

Tears streamed down her cheeks as she strode to the front door and went inside. A scream tore from her throat.

* * *

"Beth!" Doug waited for a response, but none came. He mashed the accelerator to the floor, her cry echoing in his ears.

When she'd driven off, he'd debated a whole ten seconds before rushing into the diner and coaxing the owner to share Beth's address with him. He'd felt guilty for using his status as a detective—for a second. But desperate times called for desperate measures and all that. He hated snooping into Beth's private life, but her nervousness, along with the vandalism to her car, was too much to ignore.

The hole in the tire hadn't been a fluke. The clean slice through the rubber clearly indicated that someone had taken a knife to it. Doug had kept that bit of information to himself so as to not scare the already clearly terrified woman.

The headlights of Doug's SUV pierced the dark as he turned into Beth's neighborhood. There was no mistake that the person who called Michael's phone was Beth, but why did it say TW? And why had Beth called Michael? Doug struggled to figure out how Beth connected to Michael as he sped toward her rental house. His friend lived his job. And after what happened to Christine, he'd never place a woman in danger, and taking down Tommy Wade was a hazardous goal.

The fact that Michael had her phone number

and that she called his friend sent icy fingers crawling up Doug's back. According to Michael's boss, his friend had planned a meeting with one of Tommy Wade's low-level lackeys on a rented fishing boat. The boat his friend was on blew up before the minion had gotten to the dock, and Michael hadn't reappeared since.

Doug prayed his friend had survived. Yet, he'd have called or at least gotten word that he was okay. Due to the danger of the investigation and the possible leak in the DEA, they'd promised to check in with each other once a day. And if Beth had any connection to Tommy, the woman had troubles on top of troubles.

He pulled in behind Beth's car and slammed the SUV into Park. His heart skipped a beat when he spotted the open front door. He yanked his Glock from his holster and sprinted up the walkway. "Beth!"

The lack of an answer made the hairs on the back of his neck stand at attention. He elbowed the door open to avoid adding his fingerprints and lifted his weapon. His steps faltered.

Beth stood in the middle of the living room, arms hugging her waist. Sobs racked her body, and tears trailed down her cheeks.

"Beth. Are you hurt?" Doug swept his gun to the left, then the right, doing a careful scan of the house. Torn couch cushions lay on the floor. Books and magazines scattered the living room. Beth still hadn't acknowledged his presence. Careful where he stepped, he moved to Beth's side.

Her startled gaze landed on him, and she took a swing.

He blocked her attempt and gently held her wrist. "It's me. Doug." Her sobs came harder. Clearing the house was priority, but he debated what to do with her. When her knees buckled, he put his arm around her to keep her upright.

She surprised him by leaning into him for support. "He found me."

"Who, Beth?" He stayed alert but wanted the information.

"My ex-boyfriend."

Another piece of the huge puzzle added to his mental picture. "Think you can stand?"

Wide green eyes stared at him. She nodded.

Once he was sure she wouldn't fall, he released her. "Stay here." He lifted his Glock and eased down the hall. After clearing the house room by room and finding no one lurking, he locked the front door and placed a call to his partner.

"Howard." His partner's voice eased the tension building in his neck and shoulders.

"Kyle, I have a problem."

"What's up, man?"

"Remember Beth, the new waitress from the

diner?" Doug proceeded to fill Kyle in on the happenings of the evening.

"Watch your back. I'm on my way." Kyle hung up before Doug could say *thank you*.

Unsurprised by his partner's willingness to jump in and assist, Doug pocketed his phone and joined Beth where he'd left her by the couch. "Whoever did this is gone."

The initial shock had worn off. "Th-thank you." She wiped her cheeks.

He searched for a safe place for her to sit and spotted the kitchen table through the doorway to his left. Whoever had broken in had rummaged through the cabinets, but the furniture in the kitchen appeared untouched.

"Let's go in there and have a seat." He holstered his weapon and led her to a chair.

Once seated, she blinked at him, struggling to process what had happened.

He hadn't asked but assumed since they were off duty, Kyle and Cassidy were together. Since their engagement, the two had become insepar-able. Although, Doug couldn't blame them. They both deserved the happiness they'd found together after the death of Kyle's first fiancée and Cassidy's police raid gone bad.

"My partner, Kyle, and most likely his fiancée, Cassidy, another detective with the sheriff's de-partment who works cold cases, are on the way."

Beth swung her head back and forth. "No. I have to leave. No one can know I'm here."

"If this mess is any indication, someone already knows where you live. It's not safe for you to be alone." He touched her arm. When she jolted, he removed his hand. "Please tell me what's going on."

The struggle was evident in her gaze. "I can't."

Doug considered not mentioning his friend, but the question that swirled in his mind needed an answer. Especially after the break-in. "You called Michael. I need to know why." He motioned to the disaster in the living room. "Does it have anything to do with this?"

A crease formed on her forehead, and she nibbled on her lower lip. "He's helping me."

The pit in his stomach grew. He hoped with everything in him that it wasn't with Tommy Wade's case. But his gut said otherwise.

"Why do you have his phone? Where is he?" Panic laced her words.

Doug's stomach flip-flopped. She didn't know. He hated to be the bearer of bad news. "Beth, Michael is missing… The evidence says he's dead."

"No. No. No." Arms wrapping her waist, she rocked back and forth. "Then I'm dead too."

Wait. What? Doug attempted to put the pieces together and hated the way they fit. But he refused to jump to conclusions. "What are you talking about?"

A crash came from outside the back of the house at the same time as the knock on the front door.

"Don't move!" Doug sprinted to the entrance, praying Kyle had arrived. He needed back up investigating the noise at the rear of the house.

Tabitha fought against the panic crawling up her throat. She gripped the edge of the kitchen table and closed her eyes. With Michael gone, she had no one to lean on—no one to protect her. The weight of reality pressed down on her. Her life was over.

Did she dare trust Doug? With his weapon drawn, he'd dashed from the house, protecting her from the unseen threat. And if she believed him, he and Michael were friends. But what did she know? Her horrible judgment of character had stained her life. Evident by her latest choice in boyfriends—a drug king who ordered and committed murder. Stupid and naive.

She dropped her chin to her chest and covered her face with her hands. How had her life gone so wrong? She'd never been loved, only used, starting with her father. All she ever wanted was someone to love her without abusing her love in return.

"Hi, Beth. I'm Cassidy Bowman."

Tabitha's heart rate spiked. She jerked her head up. A woman in jeans and a T-shirt stood a couple feet from her.

"Sorry. I didn't mean to startle you. I'm a cold case detective with the Anderson County Sheriff's Department. Doug and my fiancé, Kyle, are partners." Cassidy's kind smile eased her nerves a bit.

Tabitha ran the back of her hand under her eyes. A black streak of mascara smudged her skin. Wonderful, she probably looked like a raccoon. She leaned past the detective and peered into the living room. "Where's Doug?"

"He and Kyle are securing the perimeter. They'll be back soon."

Now what? Too many people—three people— now knew where she lived. Make that four if she included the person who'd destroyed her bolthole. And besides the person bent on making her life miserable, the others were detectives, of all things. She sucked in a shaky breath. No doubt they'd pry. How much should she tell them? If Tommy had Michael killed, she couldn't get anyone else involved. She refused to have anyone else's death on her hands. Plus, Michael suspected a leak in the agency. Did it extend to the sheriff's department? Michael hadn't said anything other than the DEA. She knew one thing for sure. She had to get out of here and find another place to hide.

The chair legs scraped on the kitchen floor. She stood and brushed past Cassidy. "Excuse me." Tabitha hurried to her bedroom to collect her go-bag that Michael insisted she keep ready. She flung open the closet doors and grabbed the duffel. Fingers wrapped around the webbed handle, her hands trembled. When she turned, she found Cassidy leaning against the doorframe of the bedroom. She clutched the bag to her chest. "Why are you following me?"

"I understand your impulse to run, but I highly advise you let Doug help you. He's a good guy. A little quiet and a bit of a neat freak, but he puts up with Kyle." Cassidy snickered. "So, he's top-notch in my book."

Mouth open, Doug's call from the front of the house halted her response. "Beth? Cassidy?"

"At least talk it over with us." Cassidy jerked her thumb over her shoulder.

"Do I have a choice?" Tabitha's heart rate spiked.

The crease in Cassidy's forehead deepened. "You always have a choice."

She snorted. "Yeah, right."

Cassidy's eyebrow rose.

The woman had no idea. Her life consisted of very few choices. And the ones she had made on her own… "Never mind. Lead the way." She followed the detective out of the room.

"There you two are." Doug's gaze landed on her bag, then lifted to her. "Planning on going somewhere?"

Tabitha glanced at Cassidy. "Apparently not."

Doug folded his arms across his chest. "We want to help. That's all."

Why would three sheriff's detectives want to help her unless they wanted to use her for the evidence? For good or bad. In her experience, no one did anything out of the goodness of their heart. They always wanted something in return.

Then Michael came along, and for one moment in time, he threw that theory out the door. He had wormed his way into her trust and led her to God. Maybe not everyone had an agenda. Or at least an unsavory one. Sure, he wanted the evidence, but he'd made it clear from the start that her life mattered more than his job. He was an exception—an anomaly. Because from her experiences, the negative had won out.

"Maybe." She hitched the go-bag higher on her shoulder. "What did you find outside?"

"It's good to see you again, Beth." Detective Howard nodded.

She'd met Kyle at the diner several times when he'd come in for dinner and knew him by sight.

He'd been nice enough to her. "Thank you, Detective."

"I think we're passed formal titles. It's Kyle."

"Here, let me take that." Doug wrapped his hand around the duffel strap.

Her fingers tightened on the bag. Her pulse stuttered. What if he took it and left her with nothing?

Doug's tone softened, and his grip loosened, but he hadn't let go. "It's okay. You keep it."

The man had read her mind, and she didn't like it. She reluctantly released the bag, allowing him to take it, and wrapped her arms around her middle. She eyed her meager belongings. The bag held her entire life and her safety net of cash Michael had provided her. The desire to grab it and run waged war within her.

Cassidy rested her hand on Tabitha's shoulder. "What do you think about getting out of here in case whoever did this comes back?"

She nodded. What else could she do with these three staring at her, unwilling to let her out of their sight?

"I think my place is best," Doug said.

Sweat beaded on her forehead. "Your house?" she squeaked.

God, is Doug safe? Or am I jumping into another bad situation? I wish Michael was here to tell me what to do. Her heart hurt at the thought of his death. *Please let him be alive.* Selfish—maybe. But the man was the only friend she had.

"His place has excellent security." Cassidy gave her a comforting squeeze. "Don't worry, I'll come too if that'll make you feel more comfortable."

Having another woman with her eased her worry. At least a little bit. Then again, the decision-making part of her brain had broken years ago. "I guess so." Tabitha hoped she'd done the right thing by agreeing.

"Come on. I'll drive." Doug motioned to the door.

"What about my car?" Trapping herself without a means to flee ratcheted her pulse. That's how Tommy had slowly taken away her freedom. Little by little, he'd isolated her until she had no way of escaping.

"I think it's best if you leave it here for now. We don't want to lead whoever did this—" Doug swept his hand in an arc at the living room "—to you."

"Fine." She ducked her head and walked out the door to his SUV. If the worst happened, she had God and his promise of eternity.

Doug's heart dropped to his toes as he watched Beth surrender. The submissiveness evident as she trudged to his SUV. Who had hurt this woman? It hadn't taken him long to realize that he had his work cut out to gain her trust. But what choice did he have? His gut screamed at him that Tommy Wade was the thread connecting Beth's problems and Michael's disappearance. Her comment about an ex-boyfriend sent warning signals firing in all directions. Doug prayed his assessment was wrong.

He jogged ahead with her duffel over his shoulder and opened the passenger door for her. "Have a seat. I'll put your bag in the back, then we'll be on our way."

"What about the house?" She gestured to her rental.

"Kyle called it in. He and Cassidy will stay until a deputy arrives. The crime techs will be here soon too. Once they finish processing the place, the deputy in charge will lock up."

She nodded.

Doug closed the car door, placed the duffel in the back of his vehicle, and climbed into the driver's seat.

Beth stared out the passenger window into the night and curled in on herself. She looked so small. Even tinier than her normal petite self. He'd let her have the silence because once they arrived at his house, he planned to ask his questions.

The light traffic made the drive quick. Ten

minutes later, he pulled into his driveway. "Welcome to my home."

Beth shifted and peered through the windshield at his house. "Nice place."

"Thank you. Ready to go inside?"

She nibbled her lower lip and shrugged.

He sighed. The woman had some serious trust issues, but at least she'd agreed. "Please wait here. I'll come around and open your door." With the state of her house and the fear he'd witnessed at the diner, he refused to let his guard down. The probability that whoever had broken into her place had followed them was low. He'd watched for a tail, but he wouldn't make a rookie mistake and risk Beth's life.

He grabbed her bag and opened the door for her. She slid out and strode with him up the walkway.

"Let's get you inside." He escorted Beth into the house, disengaged, and then reengaged the security system. "The couch is comfortable, but the recliner is the best. Go ahead and relax for a minute. I'll put your things in the extra bedroom." He left her to decide her preference of seats and headed to the guest room.

After placing her bag on the queen-size bed, he slipped into the hall and grabbed a towel and washcloth from the linen closet. He set those next to her duffel. Satisfied he'd provided what she'd need, he returned to the living room.

He found her in the recliner, clutching a throw pillow to her chest like a lifeline. He sat on the far end of the couch, giving her space. Clasping his hands between his knees, he leaned forward. "Beth, we need to talk. But before we do, can I get you anything?"

She shook her head. "Where's Cassidy?"

He tried his best not to appear threatening, but at six feet, compared to her five-two—maybe— he towered over her. Plus, he had no idea what triggers he might trip. "On her way. She and Kyle will stay at your house until the deputy arrives. Which shouldn't take long. They only need to turn over the crime scene. She'll come with him once the deputy relieves them."

"Okay." She nibbled on her lower lip.

Doug wanted to reach over and tug her lip free but kept his hands to himself. Instead, he let the silence linger between them. He had no clue what this woman had lived through, but his best guess? Abuse topped the list. Especially if Tommy Wade was involved.

Within a couple of minutes, Kyle and Cassidy came bustling in. His partner had a key and knew the code to the alarm system, so Doug stayed in his spot.

Cassidy flopped down on the couch close to Beth. "Sorry that took so long."

"I'll go make some decaf coffee for all of us." Kyle's gaze slid to Beth and back to Doug. "Go on and start without me."

Smart man. Doug wondered if he should join his partner and let Cassidy take the lead. But he had too many questions that needed answers.

"Thanks, honey. I know I can use some." Cassidy smiled at her fiancé. After the two had gotten engaged a few weeks ago, they were driving everyone in the office nuts with their lovebirds act.

He was happy for his friend, but being the only single guy on the team left an emptiness he hadn't expected. He pushed the thoughts aside and focused on the current situation. He had no desire to make Beth uncomfortable, yet he had no idea how to protect her from an unknown danger if he stayed silent. "You know Michael?"

"Yes." Beth glanced at Cassidy and then at her hands gripping the pillow.

He'd thought having another female in the house would help Beth feel safer. She'd relaxed a bit when Cassidy arrived, but she obviously didn't want to talk in front of her.

Picking up on the body language, Cassidy stood. "You know, maybe I should help Kyle. I'd like the coffee drinkable. And that man can make mud if someone isn't watching over him. If that's okay with you, Beth."

The woman kept her eyes lowered but nodded.

Cassidy rested her hand on Doug's shoulder as she went by and gave it a squeeze.

He appreciated his friend's support. Once Cassidy disappeared into the kitchen, he leaned forward. "She's gone. You can speak freely now."

"Can I?" Beth lifted her gaze and raised a brow.

Getting the woman to talk might be harder than he thought. "Michael and I are friends. You trusted him. I hope you'll trust me."

She scraped her teeth over her lower lip.

He'd seen it enough tonight to recognize it as her *I don't know what to do* sign.

"If he felt it important to help you, I'll help you too. I'd trust that man with my life—and have on occasion. But I do have a few questions." Doug waited for her to say something—anything.

"I guess so." She inhaled and met his gaze. "Ask. I'll answer if I can."

More like if she wanted to. He leaned against the back of the couch and rested his right ankle on his left knee. At least he'd made progress. "First, I'd like to know why your contact number on Michael's phone says TW."

Her shoulders sagged, and there she went with

her lip thing again. "He gave me a new name to use when he moved me to Valley Springs."

Well, that explained a lot. Whatever had caused Michael to hide her identity worried Doug. As a DEA agent, his friend didn't conceal someone for a minor concern. "Beth isn't your real name?"

"No." She exhaled. "My name is Tabitha."

Doug considered pushing about her last name but decided against it. "May I call you Tabitha, or do you prefer Beth?"

"I don't see how it matters now. He found me." A tear slipped down her cheek and dropped from her chin onto her lap.

Doug suppressed his urge to comfort her and forced himself to remain seated. "Since we don't have all the facts about who trashed your house, let's not make assumptions. We'll stick with Beth in public but go with Tabitha in private, if that's okay. I really want to help you, but I need to know who you're talking about. Who found you?"

The air conditioner kicked on, and Cassidy and Kyle's banter filtered in from the kitchen. But Tabitha remained silent.

She sighed. "Tommy Wade."

Doug sucked in a harsh breath. The man responsible for his wife's death. The same man he and Michael had focused their efforts on putting behind bars. The pieces fell into place, and his stomach plummeted at the lethal implications. "You're Michael's informant."

She glanced toward the kitchen, then back at him, and whispered, "Yes."

That bit of information terrified Doug, and he didn't scare easily. He'd suspected that answer, but the truth hit him square in the gut. Tommy had a reputation for using women at his whim. Treated them like possessions. Rumors had it that he believed in obedience or punishment. "Has he hurt you?"

"Not physically." She picked at the edging on the pillow. "Not more than I deserved."

Doug closed his eyes and took three deep breaths, calming his ire. He knew emotional abuse left its own horrible mark, and from her reactions, he had no doubts Wade had wielded that sword along with his fists. She'd downplayed the physical abuse, but he read the unstated facts. "I'm sorry for what he did to you."

"Thank you."

"Will you give me a quick rundown about what you had for Michael? I'd like to know what I'm dealing with." He held his breath, hoping she'd trust him enough to give him the basics.

"Michael came to me. Asked me to help him. At first, I refused. Tommy owned me. If I helped Michael, I'd pay the price, but then…" Her gaze drifted to a faraway place. "Let's just say I witnessed something, and circumstances had me saying yes to Michael. I decided to do what I could to take Tommy down. So, I collected evidence against him."

Doug sat up straight. "Where's the information now?"

She shrugged. "I'm not sure. I gave Michael everything I discovered about Tommy and the deaths related to his business. That's when he hid me in Valley Springs."

Doug stood and paced the room. He ran a hand through his hair. "Did he say where he put it?"

"No. Only that he wasn't ready to bring it to his boss yet."

He spun to face her. "Why not?" That made no sense. If he had enough to take Wade down, he would have given it to his commanding officer.

"I'm not sure. But he seemed worried that the information would leak."

Doug closed his eyes. "And Tommy escapes arrest—again."

TWO

Thursday, 6:00 a.m.

Sunlight streamed through the kitchen window, filling the room with a cheer Doug didn't possess. The coffeemaker gurgled to a stop. He poured himself a cup of the dark brew, took a sip, and exhaled. He leaned against the counter and stared into his backyard. Sleep had eluded him most of last night. The thought of protecting another woman from Tommy Wade had caused him to toss and turn until the early hours of the morning. Even then, he had a fitful rest, at best.

Thankfully, Tabitha had allowed him to bring Kyle and Cassidy into the know. And not holding a secret from his partner sent a wave of relief through him. After they'd called it a night, Tabitha's disclosure had his mind whirling in a hundred different directions. He knew one thing for sure, he had to take time off and finish what Michael had started—getting justice for those Wade had hurt.

Cassidy ambled into the kitchen, securing her hair into a messy ponytail. Blonde strands spilled from the elastic tie. He held the carafe up.

"Yes, please." She collapsed onto a chair, dropped her chin, and covered her face with her hands.

He pursed his lips to hide his smile and poured her a cup of the strong brew. "Here ya go, sleepy-head."

She peeked through her fingers.

He held out the mug, waiting for her sleep-addled brain to catch up.

She accepted the offering and took a careful sip. Her eyes closed. "Bless you."

"Does Kyle realize you're not a morning person?" He couldn't help but chuckle at Cassidy's expression.

"Bite your tongue. Don't you dare say a word. Once we're married, he's stuck with me." She sent him a playful glare and continued her infusion of caffeine.

As if Kyle had no idea. Ha. Last year, when a serial killer targeted Cassidy, Doug helped his partner with protection duty. The woman was a bear in the morning, and he and Kyle both knew it.

"Is Tabitha awake?" He wiped down the counter, tossed the wet washcloth into the sink, and returned to his spot near the window.

"I heard her in the bathroom when I got up." Cassidy's gaze met his. "She's worried that everyone knows her real name."

"I realize. We'll have to be careful in public." Doug had convinced her to allow him to explain the situation to his friends. Tabitha had reluctantly agreed. "But unless she reveals what she and Michael have done, we can't protect her."

Cassidy stared into her cup. "Keep at it. Whether she admits it or not, she trusts you."

"I'm not so sure about that." Doug ran a hand over the back of his neck. So far, he hadn't gotten that feeling. If anything, just the opposite.

"Good morning." A timid voice interrupted his thoughts. Tabitha cowered at the archway. Her toes not crossing the line to the kitchen floor.

The implications sent waves of anger rolling through him. He pulled in a calming breath. "Would you like some coffee?" He kept his tone light, hoping to relieve her fears.

"Yes, please." She didn't move from the spot at the doorway but stayed in place as if waiting for an invitation to enter.

"Come on in." Cassidy stood and held her chair out. "Take my seat. I need to head home and change before work."

"I didn't mean to run you off." Tabitha entered and accepted the seat.

"You aren't. Duty calls. I'll see you again

soon." Cassidy's gaze connected with Doug's. "Doug will take good care of you."

He nodded his appreciation. "Sure will." Mug filled, he placed it in front of Tabitha. "There you go." He opened the refrigerator, retrieved a small container of cream he kept for visitors, and placed it on the table next to the sugar. "We'll be by the office in a little while."

"I'll catch you there." Cassidy hustled out of the room.

A few moments later, he heard the security system disengage and reengage. The whole team knew his obsession with safety and always supported his paranoid quirks without question.

Doug refilled his cup and sat across from Tabitha. After a few minutes ticked by, he decided to broach last night's subject again. "Before we discuss your *situation*, I want you to know that I won't let you face this alone. I'll be with you every step of the way. However, I won't know how to proceed until I've seen what you gave Michael. So, I've been thinking—trying to figure out where Michael might have hidden the evidence. His apartment comes to mind, but I can't imagine he used such an obvious location. Then there's his locker or desk at the office. Again, if he suspected a leak in the department at the DEA, he wouldn't risk it." Doug sipped his coffee and allowed the warm liquid to ease his tension. "There's only one other place I can think of where he'd feel safe stashing the evidence."

Lifting her mug to her lips, she paused. "Where?"

"It's a private cabin that I own. Michael is the only person who knows about it."

She tilted her head. "Your friends that you work with don't know?"

He shook his head. After Christine died, he bought the place with the intention of hiding away from life. Instead, it had become his sanctuary. A place to go when he hit his stress limit, and a place to reconnect with God. At the beginning of his grief journey, Doug had pushed away from Him. *Yeah, not the smartest move he'd ever made.* But people tended to turn away instead of toward God during hard times, and he'd followed the norm. *Dumb move.* "I like having a retreat when life feels heavy."

"I can understand that." Tabitha ran her finger along the rim of her cup. "When do we leave?"

"First, I have to go to the office and ask the sheriff for time off and explain why." He chuckled. "That could get interesting."

Tabitha ducked her head. "I don't want you getting in trouble on my account."

"It'll be fine. Sheriff Monroe is a great boss and a good friend." Yeah, Dennis would understand—eventually. But breaking the news to him… Doug cringed. Up until this point, he'd kept his involvement in Michael's investigation from Dennis. That part would take a bit of finessing.

"I'll go finish getting ready. I don't want to keep you waiting."

Beyond taking down Tommy Wade's drug business and all the evil surrounding it, Doug's other goal was restoring confidence in the woman across the table. Why that meant so much, he had no idea. But he hated the fear she displayed. He placed a hand on her arm. "Breakfast first. Then we'll go. You don't have to rush."

Her muscles tightened. She stared at his hand. "If you're sure."

Realizing his mistake, he let go of her arm. "I am."

Forty minutes later, after eggs and bacon and cleaning up, Doug parked his SUV at the far end of the station's small lot. The sheriff's department hopped with activity. If you could call nine cars hopping. But for the Anderson County office, it constituted a busy day.

"Let's get you inside." He skirted the vehicle and gave the area a quick scan. Whoever had broken into Tabitha's house hadn't found what he or she was searching for. At least that's what his gut told him. He opened the passenger door and escorted her into the building.

"Morning, Detective Olsen." The sheriff's administrative assistant greeted him.

"Good morning, Brenda. The sheriff in?"

Brenda glanced at Tabitha, back to him, and raised a brow.

He had no doubt Brenda knew Beth from the diner, but he had no intention of revealing Tabitha's real name or why he'd brought her to the office. He gave Brenda a slight shake of his head.

The administrative assistant took his refusal of explanation in stride. "He's in his office pouting."

Doug laughed. "What did you do now?"

A sly smile crossed the admin's lips. "It's not my fault the paperwork has to be done."

"You're pure evil, Brenda."

She tapped her red fingernail on her lips. Her eyes sparkled with mischief. "And don't you forget it."

He rolled his eyes at Brenda's playfulness and guided Tabitha to the sheriff's office. Two chairs sat near the door. "Have a seat while I talk with my boss. I'll be just inside the door if you need anything."

"I won't move." Tabitha sat, tucked herself into the corner, and hugged her purse.

The fear in her actions gnawed at his gut. He hated Tommy even more than before. Doug stuck his head inside the office. "Knock, knock."

"Come in." Sheriff Dennis Monroe ran his fingers through his hair, leaving a strip standing on end. "I hope you've come to help."

"Sorry, Dennis. That's why you get to wear the big star."

His boss chuckled. "Right. How can I help you?"

Instead of sitting, Doug stood "at ease." The action was a leftover habit from his military days. "I'm requesting a few days off to take care of a personal matter."

Dennis leaned back in this chair and steepled his fingers. "A personal matter, huh. Does this have anything to do with a certain waitress named Beth and last night's break-in?" He motioned with his index fingers to the chair on the other side of his large oak desk.

Doug sat on the edge of the seat, ready to move if Tabitha so much as squeaked. "That's an affirmative."

"I thought so. Kyle came by earlier. Said Cassidy spent the night at your house. I'm assuming that had something to do with Beth." The sheriff raised a questioning brow.

"It did. We thought Beth would be more comfortable with another woman."

"You know I'm not one to pry." His friend grinned. The man had his hands in everyone's lives, but the guys and ladies didn't care. They appreciated Dennis's concern for their well-being. More than once, he'd stopped a disaster with a simple word or action. "We're a bit busy around here. With Keith on paternity leave and all."

"Speaking of, how are the twins?" Doug couldn't be happier for his friend.

Keith, another detective, and his wife Amy had a big surprise two weeks ago. One baby had hidden behind the other at the early ultrasound, and the heartbeats had synced, leaving everyone clueless about baby number two. The delivery became the talk of the hospital as it was not a common occurrence. In fact, it ranked high on the rare scale. According to the doctor, it happened from time to time. And since Amy had been a twin, it seemed fitting. The whole experience had thrown Keith for a loop. Rattled was an understatement. They had an eighteen-month-old son Carter who kept them busy, and now two adorable girls.

The two little dolls had stolen everyone's hearts, though. And their names—Stacey, after Amy's twin who'd been murdered, and Ellie, after Keith's mother Ellen who'd died of cancer—had brought everyone to tears.

"Last time I talked with him, he sounded like he could use a year's worth of sleep. Give them a couple more weeks. Planning for one and getting two will take some adjustments."

"If anyone can do it, it's Amy and Keith. I'm

sure Grandpa Ian hasn't missed an opportunity to help."

"That's true." Dennis leaned forward, rested his forearms on his desk, and clasped his hands together. "Stop stalling, Doug. Give me the basics."

He appreciated his boss's ability to take interest in his men and women in one breath and get down to business in the next. "First of all, Beth's real name is Tabitha Wilson. Compliments of my friend Michael Lane—"

"DEA agent?"

Doug nodded. "He hid Tabitha in Valley Springs and gave her a new identity to protect her."

Dennis's eyes narrowed. "Protect her from who?"

"That's where it gets a bit sticky. I don't think she's told me the whole truth, but what I *can* tell you is that Tommy Wade is involved."

Dennis knew all about Doug's wife and the connection to the vile drug dealer. "Okay then." His boss blew out a long stream of air. "I'll admit, I don't like you going dark where Wade is involved."

"I promise not to go off-grid. But Michael had evidence against Tommy, and I have to find it."

"As I said, I don't like it, but I get it. Any news on Agent Lane?" Dennis asked.

"No. Only that he was seen on the boat a few

minutes before it blew up, and they haven't found him."

The sheriff exhaled. "I'll grant the time off. But I expect you to call and ask for help if you need it. And please be liberal with the term *need*."

"I appreciate that. I'll be out of town for a day, maybe two. I promise to keep you up to speed." An invisible weight lifted from his shoulders. For better or worse, he wasn't alone in his search for the truth anymore.

Dennis stood and skirted his desk. "Come on. I'd like to go say hi to my favorite new waitress." The sheriff walked with him to the door and peered out. "Hello, Tabitha." Dennis kept his voice low so no one else heard Beth's real name.

Her respiration increased, and she swallowed. "Hi, Sheriff."

"Is there anything I can do for you?" the sheriff asked.

She looked at Doug's boss as if the man had asked her to jump in the lake during the winter.

"Well, if you think of anything, let me know." Dennis pulled out one of his special business cards with his personal cell number on it and held it out to her.

"I don't understand." She stared at the card like it might bite.

"We all need assistance now and again. Help. That's all. Nothing more."

She snatched the card and slipped it into her pocket. "Thanks."

"Detective Olsen will take good care of you. And he makes a good sounding board too." Dennis gave Doug a friendly slap on the back and strode into his office.

"Thanks, Sheriff." After Dennis closed the door to his office and they were alone in the hallway, Doug turned his attention to Tabitha. "I have the time off. Are you ready to search the cabin?"

"I guess so." She hitched her purse on her shoulder and followed Doug through the main office. "Why is everyone being so nice? What do they want?"

"They're nice people. No one expects anything from you." The light in Doug's brain popped on. His assessment of Tabitha made him both sad and angry. The word that described her—*used*.

She shook her head. "No. People always have an agenda."

"Not this time." He held the door open for her.

She came to a halt outside the Sheriff's Department door. "I wish I could believe that."

"Give it time. We'll convince you that we genuinely care about you and want to help."

Her jaw dropped. "You don't even know me."

"But we want to." Doug continued the path to his SUV. He glanced over his shoulder and found Tabitha staring at him. "Are you coming?"

"Fine."

Confident she'd follow, Doug held up his key fob and hit the start button.

The SUV exploded. The blast threw him backward into a parked car. He whipped forward and hit the ground. Pain burst through his body.

Flames shot from the SUV, warming his skin. His ears rang, and his head whirled. He lay on his back, staring at the sky. Debris floated in the air, and a dark haze drifted above him.

Had Tabitha survived? She'd been several steps behind him. He prayed the explosion hadn't hurt her. He wanted to get up and check on her, but his limbs and brain refused to reconnect.

"Doug!" Tabitha's voice pierced through his muffled hearing.

He shifted and lifted his head. The world tilted and swayed.

A man dressed in jeans, a black shirt, and a ski mask headed toward Tabitha. The man had a good ten inches of height on her and at least a hundred pounds. Doug had to get to her before the masked attacker got to her.

Doug struggled to his feet and staggered toward her, praying his body cooperated.

God, please send help.

Smoke swirled, and flames reached toward the sky. Tabitha stared at the blazing SUV from where the blast had knocked her to her hands and knees, the contents of her purse scattered on the ground. She'd witnessed Doug's body thrown like a ragdoll when the vehicle exploded. She hoped he'd survived and hadn't been seriously injured. Forcing her eyes from the fire scene, she located Doug. Struggling to her feet, she took a step toward him. A muscular arm wrapped her neck and choked off Tabitha's airway. Another snaked around her midsection. He lifted her off her feet and carried her toward a waiting vehicle. She clawed and kicked at the man, but his grip was too tight to escape. She hadn't seen his face. Had no idea who had her in his hold.

She prayed someone inside the sheriff's office heard the blast. Of course they had. How could they not? However, when they came outside, they'd concentrate on their friend—not her. She was nobody to these people. But she refused to give up. She had to try.

"Help!" Her scream came out as a whisper. She flailed her legs as the open car door came closer and closer. If he got her inside, she'd never be found again. Or if so, she'd be dead. She thrashed her head and sunk in her nails, slicing them across the man's skin.

A blur came from her left.

The sudden impact sent her sprawling onto the pavement. Her palms stung, and her knees ached, but she sucked in a full breath for the first time since the man had wrapped his arm around her throat. She scrambled away from the chaos, gasping to fill her lungs, and discovered Doug fighting her attacker.

The masked man landed a hard right hook to Doug's jaw and ran off down the street.

Doug ignored the attacker that fled on foot and crawled to her. He placed his hands on either side of her face. "Are you okay?"

She almost laughed. Dirt covered his torn jeans and shirt, his face bruised and smeared with grime, and his hair mussed to the point of comical. And he asked about her? "I'm fine."

He raised a brow.

"Seriously, I'm alive. I'll take it." She placed a hand on her stomach and closed her eyes. *Thank You, God.*

Sheriff Monroe, Kyle, and another man Tabitha didn't recognize came running. "Do you need an ambulance?" the sheriff asked.

Doug stood, wobbled a bit, and straightened. "No. Jason, Dennis, take Tabitha inside and make sure no one has access to her. Kyle, you're with me."

Without question, Kyle joined Doug and sprinted down the street where her assailant had vanished. She watched the two detectives disappear from sight. Her hand drifted to her throat. It was as if the bruises were forming beneath her fingertips. She swallowed and winced at the soreness.

Dennis pointed to the man next to Tabitha. "Take her to my office. Get those scrapes tended to. I'm securing the scene and calling the crime techs."

Sirens from the fire engines signaled their approach.

"On it, Boss." The man helped her to her feet. "I'm Jason Cooper. My partner Keith Young and I work with Doug."

Unsure what to say, she nodded. Tabitha looked over her shoulder, worried about Doug. He'd taken a brutal blow from the explosion. Now he was chasing the man who'd tried to abduct her.

"Doug's ex-Army and a good deputy. He knows what he's doing." Jason placed a gentle hand on her elbow. "Let's get you inside. I'd like to avoid his wrath if I don't protect you and take care of your injuries."

"He seems too nice to get angry at you." Of course, she'd made *that* mistake more than once. Not with Doug, but with Tommy and her uncle.

Jason laughed. "Doug's a quiet one, but don't let it fool you. He's a fierce protector when it comes to his friends."

"I'm not sure I belong in that category." Sure, she'd waited on him at the diner over the past couple of weeks, but did that make them friends?

Tabitha admitted Doug hadn't left her side since someone broke into her home. But friends?

The detective smiled. "Oh, I know you do. Come on." He held open the office door, and Tabitha scooted past him.

Brenda hurried around her desk. "Dear girl, are you all right?"

"Yes." The attention sent Tabitha's insecurities into overdrive. She still didn't understand why everyone was being kind to her.

Although, Michael's words flitted through her memories. The ones where he'd told her about God and had shown her kindness without expectations. Yes, he wanted help taking down Tommy, but Michael had always looked out for her safety. Were these people like him?

"Jason, get this sweet girl into the Sheriff's office. I'll grab the first aid kit." Brenda hurried off.

"Bossy much?" Jason rolled his eyes. "Come on." He motioned Tabitha toward the hall.

She hesitated. Uncertainty if she could trust the man stabbed at her. Tabitha inhaled, gathering her courage, and followed the detective's directions.

He held the Sheriff's office door open and pointed to a chair. "Have a seat. I saw you limping, and those scrapes look like they hurt."

"Maybe a little." No use denying it. Her hands and knees stung with a vengeance.

Jason snorted. "I'm guessing more than a little." He tilted his head and studied her, then knelt beside her, keeping a couple feet of separation. She'd give him kudos for not touching her. "I've heard a bit about what's going on. I'm not sure what happened in your past, but I want you to know that Doug is a great guy. He's rather a protective type. You're safe with him. With all of us."

That was the third or fourth time someone mentioned that she'd be safe with Doug. Maybe she could trust him with everything. Including her biggest secret of all—her reason for risking everything to escape Tommy—the baby growing inside her.

Brenda bustled in, waving the first aid kit. "Got it. Now, let me take a look at those injuries."

She might as well not argue with the woman. Her wounds did need tending to. Palms up, she smiled at Brenda. "I appreciate your help."

"That's what we do around here. We help people. The good Lord wouldn't want us turning anyone away."

"I guess He wouldn't." Tabitha had recently discovered her faith and still found it difficult to understand such love. Her horrible childhood had rolled into an abusive adulthood. Everyone in her past used her in one way or another. No one had ever given her unconditional love. It baffled her how a God so big loved her and all her ugly past. But she'd made the step of faith. More like a leap across the Grand Canyon.

"Beth!" Doug's voice echoed in the hallway.

Jason stuck his head out the door. "She's in here, dude. Stop shouting."

Doug rushed into the room. A purple bruise already marred his jaw where the assailant had hit him. Scrapes covered his arms and face, and he grunted when he crouched next to her. He brushed a stray strand of hair behind her ear. "Did he hurt you?"

Tears flooded her eyes. No man had ever looked at her with such compassion. Unable to speak past the lump in her throat, she shook her head. The bruises on her neck didn't matter.

Brenda closed the lid on the kit. "I'll leave the two of you alone for a bit. Come on, Jason. Scat."

"Yes, ma'am." Jason rolled his eyes and turned to Doug. "I'll gather the group."

Doug never took his eyes off her. "Thanks, Jason. We'll be out in a minute." Once the door closed and they were alone, he cupped her cheek. Shocked that the warmth of his palm calmed her instead of making her cringe, she leaned into his touch. "Are you really okay?"

"Yes. Thanks to you, but I should be the one asking you that. I saw you fly backward and hit that car. I thought…" She sucked in a sob. "I thought you were dead."

"It wasn't my time. And I'm very glad about that. Thankfully, the vehicle exploded upward and not out, limiting the damage to the surrounding cars—and us." He removed his hand but stayed by her side. "I want to help you, Tabitha. Please let me and my friends do that."

The thought terrified her, but she knew saying no meant the end of her life if Tommy got a hold of her. "I'm scared, Doug. Not only of Tommy and whoever is after me, but I don't trust easily. For some reason, I want to trust you, which frightens me more than anything."

A lopsided grin appeared on his bruised face. "I'm one of the good guys, Beth."

She tilted her head. "Why did you call me that? I mean, I understand and appreciate it when we're in public to keep people from discovering my identity, but we're in private."

"I like it. It signifies a new beginning for you. And I think you need one. But if you'd prefer Tabitha, that works for me too."

Her heart fluttered. Doug's words hit the target. Beth, the waitress, had found a life without abuse. One she lived for herself, not controlled by those around her. Even if she hid from her ex-boyfriend and lived in fear of what he would do to her, the freedom that she'd experienced gave her hope.

She ducked her head. "I like Beth."

He tipped her chin up with the tip of his finger. "What is it?"

She bit her lower lip. "I like *you* calling me Beth."

"Then it'll be my name for you." The man looked rather pleased about her statement. "I want to get to my cabin and see if we can find that evidence, but I think we should talk with my team first and make a plan. Are you okay with that?"

There it was again. Him giving her a choice. "Yes."

He struggled to his feet with a groan and held out his hand. "Come on, let's go before Jason decides to find us and give me grief for making him wait."

She accepted his gesture and stood.

He dipped his chin and peered into her eyes. "You've got this, Beth. You're stronger than you realize."

Did she have this? Was she strong? For the first time since Michael convinced her to take down Tommy, her heart quit pounding and relaxed into a steady rhythm. Thanks to the man whose powerful hand held hers.

Not waiting for a response, Doug led her out of the office. They joined the others in the conference room. He held out a chair for her. Stunned by his actions, she stared at him. When he winked at her, she smiled and sat in the offered seat.

Once Doug settled beside her, the room grew quiet, and all eyes turned to the sheriff.

"Personal leave retracted. This is an official case." Finger pointed at Doug, the sheriff scowled. "Medical attention, then I want to know why someone tried to blow up one of my detectives. There's been way too much of that going on over the past couple of years."

"Kyle has already played wannabe doctor." Doug jutted his chin toward his partner. "I'll clean up when I get home, and I promise to say something if I feel worse."

"I'm holding you to that. You, too, Tabitha."

She nodded, not knowing what else to say at the orders.

The sheriff addressed the group. "Meet up at Doug's house in an hour. I want as much information as we can gather. I know we won't have conclusive evidence, and it will be minimal at best. But I want every thought, every theory, every possibility on the table."

A round of "Yes, sir" filled the room.

Cassidy strode in, placed a hand on Kyle's shoulder, and smiled at him. Then wagged her finger between Doug and Tabitha. "I heard what happened. I'll give these two a ride home while the rest of you tackle the scene."

The tenderness in Cassidy's eyes as she peered

at Kyle made Tabitha believe it was possible for people to love each other without fear.

"Thanks, Cassidy." Doug shifted to face her. "Beth, are you ready?"

The sheriff raised a brow, but she refused to acknowledge his curiosity at the cherished way Doug spoke her name.

She lifted from the chair. "Whenever you are." Her stomach twisted in a knot at the thought of leaving the building with her attacker on the loose.

Cassidy folded her arms. "I'm taking my department-issued vehicle with all the firepower available. I'm not messing around after what happened."

"Sounds like a good plan to me." Doug placed his hand under Tabitha's elbow and nodded at Cassidy. "After you, Detective."

The three weaved through the main office to the front door. When they stepped from the building, the warm August air hit Tabitha's face. Her nerves sparked like live wires. Out in the open was the last place she wanted to be. She scanned the area, terrified her attacker lurked beyond the parking lot.

Had he circled back and waited for another opportunity to snatch her?

THREE

Thursday, 11:00 a.m.

An hour and a hot shower later, Doug eased his aching body onto the couch. Bruises had blossomed on his back and torso, compliments of the explosion. His headache had dimmed to a dull throb after the two Tylenol he'd swallowed when he arrived home. He had the signs of a mild concussion that he refused to let control him, but he wouldn't be careless either. He'd assured Dennis that he'd notify him if his condition worsened, and he intended to keep his promise.

Cassidy puttered in the kitchen while Beth joined him on the sofa. She sat with her chin down and nibbled on her lower lip. The woman kept every word, every reaction, in check. The entire time she'd stayed with him, she'd waited for an invitation to enter a room or add to a conversation and deferred to him or others on several occasions. He'd witnessed the effects of domestic trauma on the job, but never had it been as personal as it was now.

He clutched her hand and spoke low so Cassidy couldn't hear. "You're going to make it bleed."

She jerked her gaze in his direction and licked her lip. "Sorry."

"Don't apologize. You've done nothing wrong." He squeezed her hand in an attempt to comfort her. Although he doubted that he succeeded. "I don't like to see you hurt yourself."

The look in her emerald eyes made him wonder if anyone had ever cared about Beth in her life.

A slight smile graced her face.

Butterflies chose that moment to flutter in his stomach. What about this woman had him tied in knots? Yes, he missed his wife, always would. But he'd moved beyond the heartache. The guilt—that was another story. He'd dated in the last couple of years, but no one had turned his head like the timid woman beside him. However, now wasn't the time to explore the attraction or the reasoning. His focus had to remain on taking down Tommy Wade and stopping the drugs from flowing through Anderson County—and getting justice for his wife.

The front door opened. Kyle took care of the alarm, and the team streamed inside.

"Man, it's hot out there. Sure could use a drink." Jason fanned his face.

Kyle slapped him on the back. "Not very subtle, dude."

Doug shook his head at his friends' antics. When he'd moved to Valley Springs several years ago, the guys had pulled him out of his funk and became his best friends. He had no idea what he'd do without them.

"I heard that." Cassidy poked her head out from the kitchen. "I've got the iced tea, boys. Be there in a minute."

"Oh, bless you, Cassidy." Jason grabbed a couple of chairs and joined Doug and Beth.

Kyle went to help his fiancée and returned with glasses filled with ice while Cassidy held the pitcher.

Sheriff Dennis Monroe waltzed in a few minutes later and secured the door. "Glad everyone is on time." He took the offered beverage, lowered himself onto the recliner, and pinned Doug with a glare. "Before we start, I want an update on how Tabitha and Doug are doing."

Doug decided it was best to get to the point. "I'm sore, and the head's a little out of whack, but I'm good." When Beth remained silent, he nudged her.

Her scraped hand went to her throat. "Oh, I'm okay. Nothing time won't heal."

The darkening purple on her neck from where the guy had wrapped his arm and dragged her to the waiting car had Doug's blood pressure rising. The woman downplayed her injuries. Her throat and scrapes had to hurt. He thought about calling her on it but refrained.

Dennis grunted. Doug assumed the utterance was due to his boss not liking how they'd both glossed over their conditions. "Jason, what did you find out from the Sheriff's Department security cameras?"

"Not a lot. Twenty minutes before the explosion, a figure, most likely male, in dark clothes and a baseball cap pulled low over his face, walked past Doug's SUV, taking longer than necessary. The man then continued down the sidewalk. I speculate he circled back and hid in the trees along the parking lot."

"No identifying features?" Kyle asked.

"Not that I can tell, but I'm not a tech guru. Beth, what do you think? Did you recognize the guy?" Jason asked.

"I'm not one hundred percent certain, but I'm pretty sure it was Clark, Tommy's number two, that tried to take me. When I grabbed his arm, I felt a long scar. One that matches Clark's from a knife fight. But I'm not one hundred percent certain," Beth responded just above a whisper.

"I'll let the lab rats know." Jason took a sip of tea.

Dennis chuckled. "Your wife really started something."

Beth's brow furrowed. "Lab rats?"

Doug rested his hand on her arm, which didn't go unnoticed by the sheriff. "Jason's wife, Melanie, is a forensic anthropologist and our county coroner. When she first took the job, she tagged the lab techs with the moniker *lab rats*, and it's taken on a life of its own."

"And they're okay with this?" Her pitch rose to almost a squeak.

How could he explain? "It's not derogatory. We hold them in the highest regard."

Jason straightened in his seat with pride. "My wife's a force to be reckoned with. Her respect for them is beyond compare. And since she's one of the best in her field, they like the nickname because it came from her."

Dennis leaned back. "So, the lab rats have the footage, but until they study it, we have nothing concrete except Tabitha's impression."

Jason nodded. "That's a fair assessment."

"Kyle?" The sheriff shifted his gaze to Doug's partner.

"At the mention of Tommy Wade, I did a cursory search and came up with nothing more than what we all know. Businessman who runs drugs on the side. Or should I reverse that? Drug dealer and businessman on the side is more like it." Kyle shrugged. "Unless I have more to go on, I don't know where to dig."

"I spoke with the VSFD's Captain Phillips. He's had training in arson investigations, and according to him, the preliminary findings suggest that someone detonated the explosion remotely."

"You mean I didn't trigger it?" Doug hated that the whole thing happened, but the fact he hadn't caused it... His shoulders sagged with relief.

Dennis shook his head. "Captain Phillips can't confirm it without a full investigation. But they did find a good-size chunk of the detonator that has him convinced it wasn't activated by the engine starting. I'm guessing the suspect either wanted to eliminate Doug or create a diversion to abduct Tabitha."

"Or maybe both?" Kyle held up his palms.

"Kyle's right. If I hadn't turned and stopped to wait on Beth, I'd have been directly in the blast zone. And the masked man would have snatched her without an issue since the explosion would have drawn everyone's attention."

"Dude, you do know her name is Tabitha, right? It's not like we're in public, and you have to use her alias." Jason waggled his eyebrows.

"Leave it alone." He glared at his friend, then glanced at Beth. She sat paralyzed next to him.

He didn't like her pallor. Once the meeting broke up, he'd pull her aside and figure out what had caused her distress.

Jason took the hint and leaned forward. "Now what? We're no closer to figuring out exactly what we're up against. Sure, we're looking at Wade, but he's an ongoing dagger in everyone's side. Nothing new there. Can you two tell us anything else?"

Doug hoped Beth would speak up, but she refused to make eye contact with anyone on the team. What choice did he have but to spill his secret? He'd allow Beth her silence for now. But he owed it to the guys and Cassidy to give them more information. His private search was about to become public.

He exhaled. "You all know that while I was deployed, someone broke into our house and killed my wife."

Beth jerked her head up. Her wide green eyes stared at him. "What?"

Doug had forgotten that Beth knew nothing about his past. What a way to find out. He swallowed hard before continuing. "Five years ago, during my deployment overseas, my wife Christine witnessed a drug deal gone bad. Tommy Wade murdered a man in front of everyone on the street. But you know how that goes. No one *saw* anything. She was the only one willing to tell the police what had happened. They asked if she'd testify when the case went to trial, and she agreed. Two nights later, someone broke into our home and shot her—execution style."

Beth sucked in an audible breath. "I'm so sorry."

He patted her hand. "I've dealt with it. Mostly."

Dennis pursed his lips. Realization that there was more to the story flashed in his eyes. "Go on. I know part of it, but I think I need to hear the rest."

"A friend from my Army days, DEA agent Michael Lane, came to me six months ago. Said he was tired of Tommy Wade always slipping through the cracks of justice and planned to take him down once and for all. He asked if I wanted in." Doug's gaze met Dennis. "I said yes. Christine deserves to have her killer caught."

The sheriff rubbed the back of his neck. "Olsen, you know I would have supported you to work with Lane. You didn't have to go behind my back."

Doug cringed at Dennis's accusation. "It was never my intention to deceive you. And you know I trust you. But Michael asked me not to say a word about his secret investigation. Anytime he'd collected proof in the past, it never stuck. He worried that Tommy or his attorney received leaked information and fixed it before anyone could take him down. Not long after I agreed to work with him, Michael had someone on the inside gathering evidence who he had to protect." He fought the urge to look at Beth. He now knew she was the one who had risked her life to get his friend that proof.

"Do we know who Michael's source was and what he discovered?" Kyle's gaze flickered to Beth then back to him. His partner had his suspicions, but refrained from asking outright.

Doug wiped a hand down his face. Here came the sticky part. "Not completely. I have a…lead, but can't say yet."

Jason narrowed his eyes. "Can't or won't?"

"Can't. I trust all of you, and I need your help. But I'm not in a position to share that part of the story." He prayed his coworkers understood. If things got worse, he'd have to share with or without Beth's permission.

"I'll allow the undisclosed information for now. When this is over, I want the whole story." Dennis stated in an all-too-familiar, *don't argue with me* tone.

Doug nodded. His phone chimed, and he pulled it from his pocket. "Why is the Lincoln County Sheriff's Department calling?" He tapped the answer button. "Detective Olsen."

"Detective, this is Deputy Coleman with LCSD. My partner and I found a man in a remote cabin on our side of the lake. When the owners came home, they discovered him unconscious and bleeding. While they waited on the paramedics, the owners said the man came to for a moment and said your name before he went unconscious again. The guy's in bad shape. I hope he makes it."

Doug sat up straight. "Who is it?" He felt the team staring at him, but he focused on the deputy's voice.

"Unknown. We hoped that you could tell us. He's on his way to Valley Springs General Hospital since it's closer. In fact, he should be there by now. It took us a few minutes to figure out who you were and contact you. Would you be willing to meet me there?"

"Of course." Doug's mind whirled with the information. Who said his name and why? One of his confidential informants? Maybe. He rubbed his forehead with his thumb and finger. But the distance didn't compute. "I'll be there soon."

"I appreciate it. I hope you can identify our John Doe."

Doug thanked the deputy and hung up.

"Want to fill us in?" Dennis scooted forward in his chair and rested his elbows on his knees.

Doug relayed the conversation to the others. "I have no idea who the guy is that they found, but I'm heading to the hospital to try and give LCSD a name to go with their John Doe." His thoughts drifted to Michael. Could it be him? But if so, how had he ended up so far from the boat incident? He reined in his hope. And he definitely wouldn't say anything to Beth. Because the probability was slim at best.

He locked gazes with her, debating what to do. There was no way he wanted to leave her, but he'd let her decide whether to stay or come with him. It seemed the woman rarely had the opportunity to make her own choices in life. He refused to follow that same path unless her life was at stake. "Are you okay coming with me? Or would you rather stay with Cassidy?"

She stared up at him with those uncertain green eyes of hers. "I'll go with you if it's all right."

"More than." Doug stood and groaned. "I'd forgotten how sore I am." He helped Beth up. "Let's head out. We'll take my personal truck since my department vehicle is toast. Kyle, you'll lock up?"

"I've got it, man. Go." Kyle waved a dismissive hand.

"I expect an update. No more going through this alone." Dennis said.

"Promise, Boss." Doug retrieved his keys from the hook near the door, and he and Beth headed out. His instincts told him to hurry.

Cold air blew from the truck's vents, tousling Tabitha's hair. She brushed a few strands from her eyes and tucked them behind her ear. Doug's confession about his wife Christine had stolen her breath. Tabitha had thought he cared about *her*. But arresting his wife's killer topped his list. She understood—she really did. However, the realization that he needed her to complete his task sent her reeling. Just another person using her.

God, I thought he was different. Or am I wrong? I've been wrong about so many things. I don't know what to think anymore. Why did Michael have to die? I trusted him. Sure, he wanted to put Tommy behind bars. But he offered me a way out whether I helped him or not. And he led me to You.

"Beth?"

She shifted to face Doug. "I'm sorry. Did you say something?"

"I asked if you're okay. You seem awfully quiet, even for you."

"Just thinking." Tabitha returned her gaze out the window. "Do you have any idea who the mystery man is?"

"Not a clue. Deputy Coleman didn't give me much to go on." He entered the hospital parking lot and pulled to a stop. "Wait, I'll come around. I want you to stay close. We don't know who is after you." His hand hovered over his weapon as he scanned the area. A moment later, he opened her door.

She slid from the seat. "Do you think he's out there?"

"The guy who attacked you?"

She nodded.

"My guess? Yes. Either way, I'm not taking a risk with your safety." He tucked her in close, and they strode into the hospital. "Please, don't leave my side."

The sincerity in his voice had her second-guessing her judgment of Doug's motives. The man had done nothing but help her since last night, even before he knew her connection to Tommy and Michael. "I won't. I promise."

Doug led her to the receptionist's desk and presented his credentials. "Lincoln County Sheriff's Department sent in a John Doe and asked me to come make an ID."

"Let me call and find out, Detective." The receptionist lifted the phone when a nurse bustled through the door.

"Detective Olsen." The woman in blue scrubs smiled.

Doug shook her hand. "Janie. How are you?"

"Good. Glad it's not one of you boys here for treatment."

He chuckled. "Not this time. Janie, this is Beth. Beth, this is Janie, nurse extraordinaire."

"Nice to meet you, sweetie. These boys have kept me busy over the last year or two." She patted Doug on the shoulder. "I'm guessing you're here for the John Doe."

Doug cringed at Janie's touch. The poor guy's injuries probably ached with a vengeance. "Yes, ma'am."

"Come with me." Janie motioned for them to follow.

Tabitha stayed in step with Doug as they trailed Janie through the double doors.

"The man you're here for hasn't regained consciousness. Although he's shown signs of coming around, so we're hopeful. The deputy stepped away for a moment, but said he'd return in a few minutes." Janie pushed open the door to a room at the end of the hall. "Go ahead. Take your time. Please, let me know if you recognize him."

"Will do. Thanks, Janie." Doug placed his warm hand on the small of Tabitha's back and escorted her into the room.

A broad-shouldered, tall man lay under the white sheets. A stark contrast to his bruised arms and swollen face. An IV ran from the pump to the back of his left hand. And the heart monitor beeped in a gentle rhythm.

Doug slipped away from her and stepped to the bed. He tilted his head, studying the man. A sharp inhale had her hurrying to his side.

"What's wrong?"

Doug clasped the man's wrist. "It's Michael."

"What?" She leaned closer to get a better look. Her fingers covered her mouth. A whimper escaped before she could stop it. "He's alive." She prayed he'd survived. Oh, how she'd prayed, but hadn't expected her prayers to be answered.

"Stay here." Doug hurried from the room, leaving her alone with the man who'd cared enough to get her away from Tommy and point her to God.

Tabitha laced their fingers together. "Michael? Can you hear me? I really need you to wake up and tell me what to do. I'm not sure who to trust." Tears burned her eyes. She'd never had romantic feelings for Michael, only a growing friendship. And now, her friend lay in the hospital, injured and unconscious. She had to put an end to the damage in Tommy's wake. Her courage wavered, but she owed it to Michael to finish what they'd started.

The door opened, and Doug strode in. He glanced at her and Michael's intertwined hands. "I'm sorry if I interrupted."

"Not at all. I thought talking to him might help." She released Michael's hand and moved to Doug's side.

"Good idea." His entire countenance shifted to work mode. She'd seen it happen before. "I only told Janie who he is but asked her to keep it quiet."

"Shouldn't his family and boss know he's alive? And what about the deputy that found him?"

"For now, I'd like to keep Michael's identity a secret." Doug threaded his fingers through his hair.

She tilted her head and studied him. "Why? Don't you trust the deputy?"

"To be honest, I'm not sure. It all comes down to the fact that if Michael's name gets out, he becomes a target again. Someone tried to kill him once. I don't want a repeat of that. Until we get a handle on the investigation and if there's a leak, I want to keep his identity under wraps."

She hadn't considered that. "Will Janie keep your secret?"

He nodded. "I have full faith she'll stay quiet, barring anything illegal."

"What do we do now?"

"I'd like to stay for a bit and see if he regains consciousness, but searching for the evidence he hid is the top priority."

Janie rushed in. "Detective, there's a man out there acting weird."

"How so?" Doug asked.

"He's purposely hiding his face and wandering around the floor, peeking into rooms. I don't like it. Especially after what you told me."

Doug stiffened. "Stay here. Don't let anyone

come in but me." He turned to leave, and the door flung up.

Doug drew his weapon and pointed it at the man who stood at the entrance of the room. "Police! Don't move!"

The guy raised his hands in the air. "Whoa, there, cowboy. Don't shoot a brother in blue. Name's Coleman. I'm the one who called you."

"ID." Doug's all-business countenance hadn't wavered with the deputy's announcement.

Coleman removed the credentials from his pocket and held them up.

Doug squinted at the proof and lowered his Glock but didn't re-holster it. "Don't let these three out of your sight." He rushed from the room.

"Mind telling me what that was all about?" Deputy Coleman shifted his gaze from her to Janie and back.

Janie stepped forward and stood between Tabitha and Coleman. "He's checking out a possible threat in the hospital."

The detective's forehead crinkled. "Right. You're not telling me everything. But I'll accept your answer for now."

Tabitha released a long breath. *God, I'm holding on to faith that all this will be over one day. But until then, please keep us safe from Tommy and his men.*

Michael moaned.

She hurried to his side and caught herself before she used his name. "Hey, there. Go ahead and wake up." Tears stinging her eyes, Tabitha leaned in and whispered in his ear. "I need your help. I don't know who to trust."

Michael's eyelids fluttered and opened to tiny slits, then closed.

"That's it. A little more." She'd noticed that Janie hadn't moved from her position, and Tabitha appreciated the protective gesture. It had to be hard not to go to her patient.

Footfalls echoed and stopped inside the room.

She pivoted to see Coleman level his weapon on Doug, then lower it.

"Did you find him?" Janie asked.

"No. But I need to get Beth out of here. I called Jason to come help with our John Doe. He's pulling into the parking lot as we speak, he'll be at the elevators in a couple of minutes. Seems the sheriff already planned for backup." Doug closed the door and joined her at the bedside.

"I can stand guard until your man gets here if that's what you need," Coleman offered.

"I appreciate that, but I don't know you. I know Jason."

Coleman narrowed his gaze, studying Doug for a moment, then gave a quick nod. "Understood. Since this is under my jurisdiction, I want a full statement for my report. I'll be outside the door until your friend arrives." He spun and exited the room.

With Coleman gone, Doug returned his attention to Michael. "Anything?"

"Yes, he's coming around. Do we have a few more minutes?" She wanted to talk with Michael and make sure he would be okay.

"A few, but not much more than that." Doug placed his hand on Michael's arm. "Come on, buddy. Wake up."

Several minutes later Michael stirred.

"Michael, please." Tabitha knew how ridiculous it sounded to beg, but she couldn't help herself.

"Beth?" His voice was so soft she thought she'd imagined it.

She leaned in close to his ear. "I'm right here. So is Doug."

Michael forced his swollen eyes open. His unfocused gaze wavered then pinned Doug. "You have to take care of her." His words slurred.

Doug placed a hand on Michael's blanket-covered leg. "I am, my friend."

Michael's gaze drifted back to her. His eyelids drooped. "I heard you earlier." He licked his dry lips. "You can trust Doug."

She swallowed the lump in her throat and squeezed his hand. "Okay."

"Not…seems…eviden…" Michael lost consciousness again.

"Michael?" When he didn't respond, she faced Doug. "What did he mean by all that?"

"I'm not sure. But I do know we have to go. The quicker we find that evidence, the better." Doug joined Janie near the door. "He's in danger."

"I'll take care of hiding him. New room. New name, if anyone asks." Janie pulled out her phone and sent a text message. "Let Jason know, Nick Jackson. Room 303."

Doug narrowed his gaze. "Wait. That's maternity."

Janie winked. "Exactly."

"You're a crafty woman, Miss Janie."

The nurse laughed. "Now get out of here and distract Deputy Coleman so I can get our friend upstairs."

Doug clasped Tabitha's hand. "Ready?"

Was she? Not really. Michael said she could trust Doug. So far, the man had proven himself, so she'd listen to Michael—for now. "Whenever you are."

They headed for the door, and her steps faltered.

Doug placed his hands on her shoulders, dipped his chin, and peered up at her. "What's wrong?"

"Do you think he's still out there?"

"The man Janie spotted?"

She nodded.

"Honestly, I don't know. But we can't assume he's not." He gave her a lopsided smile and jerked his head toward the exit. "Come on."

She continued down the hall, tucked in next to Doug.

Had the suspicious man come for Michael, or had he followed her to the hospital, ready to try to abduct her again?

FOUR

Thursday, 4:00 p.m.

Michael was alive. *Thank You, God.*

Doug's hands tightly gripped the steering wheel as he forced the tension streaming through his body into a manageable box. The tires hummed on the highway, and the air conditioner hissed, struggling to cool the interior of the vehicle in the August heat. With Michael slipping in and out of consciousness, Doug had to rely on his gut to discover where his friend hid the evidence. And the cabin topped the list. Ha. Who was he kidding? It made up the entire list. If it wasn't there, he had no clue where to look.

He glanced at Beth then back to the road. She hadn't said a word since they left the hospital. He thought he'd made progress in the trust department, but apparently, he was wrong. Either that or he'd done something that caused her hesitation— again. "I know I keep asking, but are you okay?"

"Yes." Her gaze didn't waver from the passing scenery out the passenger window.

"The doctors and nurses taking care of Michael are top-notch. He's in good hands."

She nodded. "I could tell."

Wow, getting her to have a conversation was harder than he thought it would be. Especially after Michael told her to trust him. Giving up for the moment, Doug tapped the speed dial on the truck's dash screen.

"Sheriff Monroe."

"Hey, Dennis." Doug glanced at his rearview mirror. Nothing out of the ordinary, but with the curves in the road, it was hard to tell. He'd stayed alert as they'd exited the hospital, but worry niggled at him.

"Doug, I'm glad you called. Jason's at the hospital standing guard outside Agent Lane's room, but I haven't talked with him since he arrived. What's the update?"

"Nothing more than what you probably already know. Michael woke up for a moment. Janie's keeping his identity under wraps. Beth and I are heading to a cabin where I think Michael might have hidden the evidence against Tommy Wade."

"You need anything from me?" He heard Dennis shuffle papers in the background.

"Eyes on Wade would be nice. And his sidekick Clark." Sweat beaded on Doug's upper lip at the idea of the sleazy businessman and drug dealer targeting Beth. He adjusted the vents toward his face to chase away the unwanted warmth.

"I sent a message to Cassidy and got an update. She's tailing Wade now over in Brentwood."

He exhaled. One less problem for him to worry about. "Good."

"Doug, I know I don't have to say it, but be careful. We don't know for sure it's Tommy behind the attempts on Tabitha."

She snorted and crossed her arms over her chest.

"Maybe. Maybe not. But I can guarantee he's not happy she escaped his clutches. What about his second-in-command, Clark? Any news on him?"

"We've got nothing yet. I have deputies searching for his whereabouts, but no one has seen him. We'll keep looking. Brentwood PD is cooperating. They want the whole group taken down."

"Clark came into the café yesterday. My guess is that he can't be far, plus Beth thought the man who grabbed her might be Clark. Let me know when you find him."

"You know I will. Check in frequently, or I'll send the guys to hunt you down."

Doug chuckled. "I'll call later."

"Keep your head on a swivel." Without waiting for a response, Dennis hung up.

"He doesn't think it's Tommy?" Beth angled toward him.

"Dennis is a great sheriff. He's covering all the possibilities. But to answer your question, most likely, he agrees that it's Wade or one of Wade's minions after you, but he, like the rest of us, won't assume. That could prove deadly if we don't look at all the angles. We want proof that Wade's our guy behind everything."

Beth nibbled on her thumbnail. "I'm sorry for shutting you out. I've never had anyone, except Michael, who hasn't wanted something from me."

"I'm sorry to hear that." Doug wondered, not for the first time, what this woman had lived through. "Maybe someday you'll confide in me and tell me what happened to you. But I understand that I have to earn your trust."

She closed her eyes, exhaled, then shifted her gaze to him. "I'm sorry if I offended you."

"Nothing of the sort. I'm not sure about all the details of your past, but I suspect your life with Tommy wasn't pleasant. That in and of itself is enough to be leery."

"You could say that." She returned her gaze to the road. "When I realized who—or should I say what—Tommy was, I found myself in too deep to walk away. People leave Tommy in one way. A body bag."

"And that's when Michael approached you?

When you wanted to escape?" Doug slowed a bit to navigate the curve.

"More or less. Granted, he wanted me to collect evidence against Tommy, but he never made me feel as though his job was more important than I was. He helped me in so many ways."

Doug drummed his thumbs on the steering wheel. "I've known Michael for years. He's a great guy."

"That he is." She rubbed her arms.

"Are you cold?"

She shook her head.

He hit a long stretch without the bends in the road. A dark-colored SUV Doug had noticed several miles back picked up speed as it exited the curve. The hairs on the back of Doug's neck stood at attention. He hit the speed dial.

"Monroe."

"Dennis, I have a tail, and he's gaining on us." Doug hit the accelerator.

"Location?"

He rattled off the highway and mile marker.

"Hang tight. Help's on the way."

The SUV edged closer.

Doug jabbed the end button. "Hold on, Beth!"

The vehicle chasing them slammed into their rear bumper.

A second hit sent them careening off the road. Beth's screams filled the cab. The truck bounced over ruts. Doug fought to maintain control, but the effort was useless. The front driver's corner of the vehicle crashed into a tree, whipping him forward. Stopped only by the cut of the seatbelt across his chest and shoulder and the exploding airbag. The teeth-jarring jolt sent his head slamming into the side window.

Doug blinked, attempting to clear the foggy haze from his brain. The truck engine hissed, spurting steam from the hood. A dusting of white powder covered the interior, and the deflating airbag hung like a popped balloon from the steering column. He turned his head, his action sluggish.

The metal of the passenger door popped and creaked open.

A tall male stood at the opening. He flicked a knife across the seatbelt then grabbed Beth by the arm, wrenched her from the vehicle, and dragged her away from the wreck.

"Doug!" Beth kicked and screamed.

He yanked on the driver's side handle, but the door refused to budge. He growled in frustration. He twisted in his seat. "Beth!"

The man hauled Beth across the ground and up the small embankment toward a waiting vehicle.

Doug fumbled with the seatbelt latch, and the mechanism released. He crawled over the console and tumbled out the passenger door. The aftereffects of the crash muddled his brain, but he pushed forward. On his hands and knees, he staggered to his feet and hurried up the slope. He had to save Beth before the attacker got her in the car. If not, knowing Tommy, she was as good as dead—or she'd wish she was.

A strong arm wrapped around Beth's waist and another across her shoulder. Her feet dangled as her abductor carried her up the slight bank toward his waiting car. She struggled against the man's tightening grip. Fear shot through her body as if lightning had struck her spine. If he succeeded in stuffing her in his vehicle... No, she couldn't go there.

"Doug!" She kicked and flailed, trying anything to escape her attacker's hold. She hadn't seen his face, but he seemed familiar. She gagged at the nasty cologne that reminded her of Clark. She had no doubt that Tommy ordered his men to bring her back ever since Agent Lane had helped her disappear.

"Beth!"

Tears streamed down her cheeks at Doug's frantic tone. Why had she ever said yes to the first date with Tommy Wade? Throughout her life, she'd gone from one horrible situation to another. But Tommy topped them all.

A dark blue SUV loomed ahead. Her heart rate skyrocketed. She refused to get in that car.

Even if the man killed her in the process, it'd be better than Tommy's brand of loyalty training. Her mind scrambled for a plan, but her options were limited. She latched on to one and forced herself to go limp.

The sudden weight change threw her assailant off-balance. She kicked backward and slammed her heel into the man's shin.

The action forced him to loosen his hold, and she scurried to escape.

Doug rushed in from her right and tackled the man to the ground, taking her with them. She landed on her back—hard. Air whooshed from her lungs, accompanied by a series of pops down her spine.

The men scuffled next to her. Fists smacking against flesh made her stomach roil. She wanted to help, but she couldn't catch her breath.

A moment later, the SUV sped off, and Doug's battered face appeared above her. She gasped, but her lungs refused to cooperate.

"Beth, what's wrong?" His worried gaze sent another wave of tears.

"Can't breathe. Back popped." Had she damaged her spine? She hadn't thought so, but the cracking sound her back had made sent nausea swimming in her belly.

Doug did a quick assessment of her injuries

and slipped her fingers into his grasp. "Squeeze my hand."

The tentacles of fear enveloped her, threatening to squash the life from her. She choked out a sob, afraid of either excoriating pain or the lack of ability to move her muscles.

He brushed the hair from her forehead with his free hand. "It's okay. I've got you."

Beth closed her eyes and tightened her grip. A wave of relief poured over her when her fingers moved.

"There ya go. Now, wiggle your toes."

She followed his directions and moved her feet. For the first time since she'd hit the ground, breathing became easier. She exhaled. The terror subsided, and her panicked thoughts disappeared.

"I think you got the wind knocked out of you. And by the sounds of it, you shouldn't need a chiropractor anytime soon." He grinned. "But I'll feel better once the paramedics assess your injuries."

Beth rolled her head from side to side, testing her neck. "No. I'm good." She pushed to sit.

Doug laid a hand on her shoulder. "Please, lie still."

"I'm fine. I'm sorry I worried you. I got scared, that's all." She sat up and cataloged her scrapes and bruises. Then took a long look at Doug. "Your jaw and cheek." Red marks covered his skin.

"Just a few bruises. And most are from the accident."

"More than a few." He'd stopped the man from taking her and probably saved her life. "Thank you."

Doug's mouth opened. Sirens wailed in the distance, cutting off whatever he'd planned to say. "Sounds like the guys are on the way."

"Help me up." She held out a hand.

"Are you sure?" The tilt of his head and the doubt flickering in his gaze touched her heart. When had anyone ever worried about her?

"Positive." When she couldn't catch her breath, and her back popped, she'd panicked. Now that she'd had time to think clearly and relax, her body had recovered, and her fears had dissipated. He clutched her hand and helped her to her feet.

She stood and swayed.

Doug's hand shot out and steadied her. His eyes narrowed. The man wanted to say something but kept his thoughts to himself.

"I guess I'm a little shakier than I thought. Let's go talk with your friends." Beth hoped her legs wouldn't betray her and add more concern to Doug's already worried features.

He nodded and followed her the final few feet to the road.

The sheriff's vehicle skidded to a stop, and

Dennis shot from the driver's seat. "Are you two okay?"

Doug placed his hand on the small of her back. "We're fine. Although, I'd like to have Beth looked over by the paramedics."

"Not going to happen." She gritted her teeth. His persistence had hit a nerve. For the love of everything, she could make decisions for herself. Those around her had dictated her entire life in one way or another. She wanted off that roller coaster. The direction of her thoughts froze her in place. For the first time ever, the mousy, scared girl cowered away, and a strong woman emerged.

Doug studied her, then sighed. "Never mind." He proceeded to fill Dennis in on the crash, and her attempted abduction. "We'll go ahead and continue to locate the evidence, but we'll need a different car." He pointed to the tangled metal. "That one is a mangled mess."

Dennis held up a finger and lifted his phone to his ear. "Hey, Kyle. Your partner needs new wheels… Okay, sounds good." He hung up. "Kyle's on his way. He said you can borrow his truck."

"I appreciate the assist." Doug swiped a hand down his face and winced when his fingers touched the bruises.

"After what happened, I want you to check in every hour." Dennis held his palm up to stop

Doug's argument. "A simple text will do. Enough for me to know that all is good."

Doug agreed and turned to her. "I'll retrieve our things from the car before Kyle arrives, so we're ready to go."

She watched him jog down the small slope.

"Is there anything I can do for you, Tabitha?" Dennis pulled her attention away from Doug.

"No." She rubbed her arms, chasing away the chill. Not from the temperatures but from her close call with whoever tried to take her. "How did they find us?"

Dennis shrugged. "I'm not sure. Doug's good at what he does. He would have noticed a tail when you left town. I'm puzzled by that."

Beth's gaze drifted to the man who'd protected her since Tommy's second-in-command, Clark, entered the diner. Doug hadn't demanded information from her, nor had he disrespected her. Instead, he'd saved her life and had stuck by her side. Plus, Michael Lane said she could trust Doug. She had a decision to make. And this time, she'd make it without anyone influencing her—unlike the other times in her life.

Doug joined them and handed her the small backpack she'd switched to using as a purse after the explosion. It contained extras like lip balm, granola bars, and such, but the important things like her driver's license and a small amount of cash were in her pocket. A habit Michael had ingrained in her.

"I know how they found us." Doug waved a little black box in the air. "Tracker."

Her jaw dropped. "When? How?"

"No clue. It had to have been at the hospital. But we don't have to worry about that happening again when Kyle gets here. No one knows we're using his truck." He tossed the tracker encased in a plastic bag to Dennis, who caught it midair. "See if the lab rats can get any prints from that."

"Will do." Dennis tucked the evidence into one of the many pockets of his black tactical pants.

Doug stepped next to her. Protectiveness oozed from his stance.

A truck rumbled up and parked behind Dennis's SUV. Kyle jumped out. "Doug, I thought I taught you how to drive better than that."

Doug's eyebrow arched. "You, teach me? Keep telling yourself that."

"I called the tow company on my way. Dennis and I will take care of the scene while the two of you find that evidence." Kyle rested a hand on Doug's shoulder and jutted his chin at Doug's swollen face. "And next time, try ducking."

"Right." Doug rolled his eyes.

Beth bit her lower lip to hide her smile. She loved the easygoing banter the men had with each other. It tugged at the tension she'd lived with for so long, loosening the knots. Was this how people lived? She'd never had normal in her life—ever.

"Are you sure you don't need medical attention?" Doug asked.

She nodded. "I'm sure." Worry about her baby niggled at her, but if they didn't find the evidence before Tommy found her, none of it would matter.

"All right then, let's get out of here." Doug motioned toward the replacement truck.

The men's conversation was background noise to the loud crunch of her shoes on the gravel. She glanced over her shoulder at the remains of Doug's truck. The accordioned engine startled her. Her heart picked up speed at what could have happened. God had watched over them, of that she had no doubt.

She slipped onto the passenger's seat of the borrowed truck and leaned her head against the headrest. Doug shut her door and half jogged, half hobbled to the driver's side.

As he pulled onto the road, he waved at his friends and headed toward the mysterious cabin he'd referred to.

Beth twisted to face him. "Do you think the person who ran us off the road knows where we're going?"

"No. Only Michael knows about it. And I called Dennis and told him before we left the hospital, but he'll keep the information to himself. The property is under a trust I set up years ago, so it's not easy to link to me but not impossible either."

"Tommy has ways of finding out information." The man had informants everywhere.

Doug nodded. "If they want to find it, they will. Hopefully, the layers will buy us a day or two to search the cabin and get back to town before anyone is the wiser."

She twisted the hem of her shirt. Doug was taking her to his private property, which even his partner didn't know about. He trusted her. The sensation, an oddity. But she owed him a token olive branch. Time to trust him—at least with the basics. "I'm sure you've noticed that trust doesn't come easy for me."

He chuckled and clasped her hand, stopping her fidgeting. "Yeah, I think I figured that one out."

The touch startled her, but the tenderness melted her apprehension. "I never knew my father, and apparently, neither did my mother. One of many on the carousel in and out of her apartment." That particular carnival ride hadn't ended after Tabitha's birth either. "She put up with me until I turned three. Apparently, a child didn't go well with her lifestyle. She shipped me off to my uncle." The mention of the man sent repulsion shooting through her veins.

"That must have been safer than living with your mother and all those men."

"One would think." She chewed on the inside of her cheek. "You know the old saying, *out of the frying pan and into the fire*?"

He nodded.

"That's putting it mildly. My uncle was an abusive monster. My mother discarded me like garbage, and my uncle used me as a punching bag." Her gaze drifted out the side window at the passing trees. "And other things."

Doug muttered under his breath words too low for her to understand. He tightened his grip, giving her the courage to continue.

"I just wanted to be loved." A tear snuck out and trailed down her cheek. She returned her attention to Doug. "I survived my uncle and got out of the house once I turned eighteen. Although, that wasn't much better. I lived on the streets for two years, hopping from homeless shelter to homeless shelter. I had a job but not enough money to pay rent. When I met Tommy, I thought he truly loved me. I saw him as a way out of my nightmare. Boy, was I wrong about that." Her stomach roiled.

"When did you realize the truth about him?"

"I'm ashamed to say it took me a couple of years to figure out his true business. But at that point, I had no way out. For all intents and purposes, I was his property."

"What made you decide to take the leap and get away?" Doug's gaze drifted to the rearview mirror and back to the road.

Having his attention elsewhere made it easier to tell him about her grisly past. "I witnessed him kill someone who dared to disobey him. That's when I knew I had to leave." Tabitha debated whether to tell Doug about the life growing inside her but chose to keep that part of her story a secret. She'd come a long way in believing that he wouldn't betray her, but the doubt continued to linger. "I had no one to turn to. I had no faith to lean on. So, I was stuck—until Michael came along."

"Did he approach you or the other way around?" Doug kept his questions to a minimum but interjected one every once in a while. His lack of interference kept her thoughts on track. The man must be good at witness interviews.

"While out shopping one day, I took a risk. I found a phone inside a women's dressing room area and made an anonymous call to the police department. They forwarded me to a DEA officer."

"Michael."

She nodded. "He promised to help me and encouraged me to meet with him. I agreed." Something about the concern in Michael's voice had spoken to her.

"Then what happened?"

"It got a bit tricky since Tommy's crew rarely let me out of their sight. But Michael came up with a plan. He gave me the name of a doctor and told me to make an appointment. When the nurse took me back to the exam room, I found Michael waiting on me."

Doug grinned. "I'll give him kudos for that plan. How often did you meet?"

Tabitha glanced out the window and inhaled, praying Doug didn't ask too many questions. "Every month, I'd make an excuse and go in for an appointment. Michael would be there, and we'd exchange information. A couple weeks ago, he helped me escape. I've hidden out in Valley Springs per his instructions. But then he disappeared...and well, you know the rest." Most of it anyway.

The hum of the engine filled the otherwise silent cab of the truck. Doug's lack of comment sent chills through her. Had she said too much? Did he even believe her? She nibbled on her thumbnail, hoping she hadn't made a huge mistake.

Thick trees surrounded them as they drove deeper into the woods. The scenery reminded her of a horror show where the too-dumb-to-live heroine trusted the wrong person, and the man murdered her in the middle of nowhere.

A nervous chuckle escaped. "Where does this road lead?"

"I've never explored beyond the turnoff, so I'm not sure."

"What turnoff?" She leaned forward, searching for a path among the trees.

The truck slowed, and he turned left down a concealed dirt road. Branches climbed toward the sky on both sides. She glanced at Doug.

His back straightened, and his eyes shifted from the rearview mirror to the side mirrors.

"What's wrong? Is someone following us?" Tabitha twisted to look through the back window. She'd been so lost in her story that she'd quit watching for a tail.

"Not that I've noticed."

"Then why are you all tense?"

"I don't want any surprises. This is my private drive." He pointed in the distance at a small cabin. "And that's my little hideaway."

Tabitha relaxed for the first time since they'd left town. "It's beautiful out here."

"One of the reasons I bought it." A few moments later, he pulled in front of a one-story log cabin with a front porch. "Welcome to my sanctuary."

"Thank you for sharing this with me. I know

you only brought me here to find the information you think Michael hid, but you didn't have to bring me along."

He shifted in his seat. "With Tommy Wade involved, I'm not letting you out of my sight." He exited the driver's seat.

Tabitha slid from the passenger side and met him at the front of the truck. Doug's hand moved to his side and rested near his weapon.

Her heart raced. "You think we aren't alone."

He shook his head. "It's not that. If they can figure out where we are, it'll take them a hot minute to find the property. I'm just edgy after everything that's occurred."

Oh, she got that all right. Edgy didn't begin to describe the twists and knots inside her. The shrubs and trees surrounding the small home made for an excellent place for a person to lie in wait.

FIVE

Thursday, 6:00 p.m.

The birds chirping in the background and the rustle of brush eased the tension that gripped Doug. The sounds of wildlife confirmed no one of the two-legged variety lurked in the woods. He held his Glock at his side, scanned the area out of caution, and motioned for Beth to join him. They traipsed up the small dirt path and climbed the three wooden steps onto the porch of the rustic cabin. He'd kept the outward appearance clean but primitive. He had no desire to invite unwanted guests to vandalize or loot his second home.

Beth's gaze ran over the faded wood exterior. "I really hope this place has running water and not an outhouse."

He snorted. Oh, it had that and more. "I think you'll be pleasantly surprised." Doug holstered his weapon and retrieved the keys from his pocket. His head pounded from the accident, and his muscles protested. Not to mention, his stomach had found empty over an hour ago. They had to find the evidence, but he hoped to have a few minutes to relax and eat before searching his little getaway.

After one more quick visual sweep of the area, he slid the key into the lock and opened the door. The familiar beep pulsed in the interior of the cabin. "Come on in." Beth entered, and he shut the door behind her. He moved to the control panel, disarmed the security system, and rearmed it. He flipped on the lights and spun to face her. "I think you'll be comfortable."

Her wide eyes took in the living room. "Wow."

A grin spread across Doug's face. The outside of the building looked like a simple hunting cabin. But the inside...a modern vacation home, with all the luxuries a person could want. "Not what you expected?"

"Not at all." Beth ambled to the kitchen at the left of the living room and ran her fingers along the granite countertop. She glanced up and smiled. "This place is amazing."

He shrugged. "You're the first person to visit except for Michael."

"I know you didn't intend to invite me, but I'm honored nonetheless." Beth walked around his sanctuary, taking in the space. "It's gorgeous, Doug."

"Thank you." He pointed to the hall opposite the kitchen. "The bedroom and bathroom are in that direction." He'd keep the underground second bedroom to himself. No need to let her in on that little secret. Not unless unwelcome company came to visit. After a quick look at the security monitors hidden in one of the kitchen cabinets, he exhaled. "We got away clean, and no one has found our location—so far. I don't know about you, but I could use a minute." His head pounded from smacking the side of his truck when the jerk ran them off the road. And his body reminded him of that ensuing collision with every step he took.

Tabitha chewed on her thumbnail. "Do you really think we're safe?"

He moved to the freezer and pulled out a container of premade pulled pork and two frozen hamburger buns. "For now." He pointed to the bar stool next to the counter. "Have a seat." He placed the pulled pork in the microwave and hit defrost. "Dinner will be ready in a bit."

"Thanks. With everything going on, I didn't realize I was hungry until now." She slid onto the barstool, placed her elbows on the counter, and rested her chin in her palm.

While the pork cooked, he sent a quick text to Dennis, informing his boss that they had arrived safely. He and Beth chatted about little things.

Favorite foods, TV shows, books. Nothing too heavy until the microwave beeped. He plated their meal, placed it on the bar, and sat next to her. They ate in companionable silence. Once finished, they cleaned up and moved to the living room.

He lowered himself onto the couch and patted the cushion next to him. "Relax for a minute before we start searching. I'm sure you ache as much as I do."

She studied him a moment, then joined him but took the far side of the sofa. Her fingers brushed the cut on her forehead. "I have to be honest. A nap sounds amazing."

Doug rolled his head to look at her. "Sorry. The best I can do is a few minutes of rest. We can't stay long. I'd like to be gone before sunup. I don't trust Tommy's crew. My guess is they'll discover the cabin quicker than I'd like."

"I'm sorry about that. Your sanctuary will no longer be private."

Yeah, he hated that fact, but for whatever reason, it didn't bother him as much as he thought it would. He felt a strong pull toward Beth and wanted to do everything in his power to help. He took a long, hard look at her. The woman was a walking contradiction. A scared little mouse on the outside. And who could blame her after what she'd confided in him? But if he peered into the depths of her green eyes, a tiger lived inside. She'd grabbed hold of Michael's offer and planned to take Tommy Wade down. That took guts—a lot of them.

"I probably shouldn't be so stingy about this place. It'd make a great weekend getaway for my friends." His gaze drifted to the wooden beams above. He'd come a long way from the broken man who'd purchased and renovated the secluded cabin.

Beth shifted and tucked her leg under her. "Did it help?"

His gaze drifted to her, and he scrunched his forehead. "What?"

She waved a hand, indicating the cabin. "Coming here."

The memory of Beth sharing her story tugged at him. She'd opened up about her past. And not an easy one at that. He owed it to her to share. "When I bought this place, it needed a lot of work. For the first week, I sat in a lawn chair and stared into the woods. No desire to do anything. My world had imploded. I was a security specialist, and someone had broken into my home and murdered my wife. The worst part… I wasn't there to protect her."

"It's not your fault. Tommy is vicious. If you'd have been there, you'd be dead too."

"At the time, I'd wished that was the case."

During those first days, he'd felt as if he was the walking dead. Not a pleasant memory. He'd had many discussions with God and hated to admit it, but he'd yelled at the Big Guy multiple times over those first few weeks until his anger settled into hurt.

"Doug." She touched his arm, pulling him from his wayward thoughts.

He shook his head. "I know. But the pain…" He blew out a breath. "It consumed me. After I climbed out of the pit of depression…" And boy, had it felt like climbing Mount Everest. "I made a commitment to myself and Christine that I'd find the man who'd killed her and make him pay."

"You're still searching for the proof that Tommy ordered the hit?" Beth had asked but stated what they both knew. "And that's why you need me." Her shoulders drooped.

"Yes, and no." How did he make her understand without adding to her hurt? "You and I have the same goal. Taking down Tommy. But I'm not using you, if that's what you think."

Head down, she peeked up through her lashes. "Are you sure about that?"

"Positive." He hated that she questioned his motives. But he understood where her hesitancy came from—Tommy had abused her and used her like everyone else in her life. He ran his fingers through his hair. His intentions came from more than a necessity to take down Wade. It came from feelings he'd yet to unpack. Might as well be honest, though. "When I saw you bolt from the diner, all I thought about was helping you. Then someone tried to take you from me, and something inside me clicked. I care about you, Beth. And I haven't cared about a woman as more than a friend in a long time."

Beth sat wide-eyed. She opened her mouth then closed it.

Doug chuckled. "Yeah, I know that feeling. Surprised me too. Look, I didn't say that to make you uncomfortable. I'm just telling it like it is."

She nibbled on her lower lip. "Michael's the only friend I've ever had."

He extended his arm and laid his hand, palm up, on the cushion between them. She slipped her fingers through his. A smile tugged on his lips. "Well, consider yourself having two friends now." And maybe more once they put Wade behind bars—possibly. Oh, who was he kidding? He'd love to explore *more* with the woman beside him.

"I like that."

Doug still saw worry lurking within her but considered her gesture a win. Beth deserved a few positives in her life. "Now that we've settled that, we should get busy searching for the evidence you gave Michael."

"Assuming it's here, it shouldn't be hard to find. This place, like your house, is immaculate."

"A gift from my Army days and, according to my therapist, a way to control the world around me when things went sideways." Christine's death had sent him into a tailspin. Controlling his environment had become essential for his sanity.

"Makes sense." Beth stood and pulled him to his feet.

The world chose that moment to tip on its side. He grabbed the arm of the couch to prevent himself from falling flat on his face.

"Whoa. Maybe you should sit back down." Beth held onto his arm, steadying him.

"Nah, I'm good. I stood up too fast. For a moment, I forgot all about the hit to my head." He tested his balance then let go of his safety net. "You start in the kitchen, and I'll take the living room. Then we'll move to the other end of the cabin and check the bedroom and bathroom." He paused and turned to her. "I'm guessing we are looking for a flash drive. Unless you have other information."

She shook her head. "I saved it in the drafts of an email he set up. It's not out in cyberspace. I'm assuming he put it on a flash drive and deleted the file since it wasn't there the last time I checked it."

"Then let's get to it."

They searched in silence, not missing any tiny hole or hidden compartment.

Doug lifted the curtain to the front window. Dusk had fallen, and darkness threatened to take over. His gut screamed at him that he'd wasted too much time recovering from the accident. They had to hurry before Tommy's men discovered the cabin, but he had to find the proof Beth gave Michael. He wanted Tommy behind bars more than taking his next breath.

Christine deserved justice, and Beth deserved freedom.

Tabitha blew air through pursed lips, chasing away the tendrils of hair that had escaped her ponytail from her face. Doug had remained quiet during the thirty minutes they'd scoured the living room and kitchen. Tension radiated off him, skyrocketing her unease. Her gaze drifted to the windows. She checked for unwanted company, but nothing appeared amiss.

She glanced at Doug. He'd offer her friendship. Not something she excelled at, but grateful nonetheless. Could she trust this man? Michael did. The decision to extend the effort of friendship ramped up her pulse rate.

God, I'm so far out of my element I have no idea what's right. Can I confide in him?

No words drifted from the air nor had quiet whispers met her ears. But a wave of certainty washed over her. Unaccustomed to sharing with others, she warred with herself what to say. She had more secrets than a government agency. Things Doug needed to know…but not yet. She couldn't go there.

"I'm not great at this get-to-know-you thing, but I'm willing to try." Tabitha closed a kitchen drawer and moved to the next one. "What are your dreams for the future?"

Doug's head popped up from where he searched near the fireplace. "Excuse me?"

"Your future. Have you ever thought about getting married again?" She ran her fingers along the inner edges of the drawer.

He released a long breath. "I've thought about it, but let's just say I haven't found the right woman."

"So, do you date?"

He chuckled. "What is this? Twenty questions?"

"Maybe." Tabitha shrugged and continued her quest. "I'm curious."

"I've tried dating. It's never worked out."

"Too many memories?"

"No. Not really. I moved past that a couple of years ago. I've just never found anyone that's caught my attention." He rubbed at the corner of his eyes. "I don't know. Maybe I'm not ready to believe I won't fail another woman."

"I understand that. I haven't made the best choices when it comes to men during my life. So, I worry that I won't be able to trust my judgment."

Doug shifted and studied her. "Kind of a pair, aren't we." He wasn't wrong.

She bit back a smile.

He motioned toward the hallway. "There's nothing in here. Are you done?"

"Just finished." Tabitha straightened and arched her back, stretching her sore muscles.

"Then let's move to the bathroom and bedroom." He peered outside before heading down the short hall.

"Did you see anything?"

"No, but my skin is crawling. I think we should hurry. I don't want to stay too long. You take the bathroom. I've got the bedroom."

She nodded and hustled into the small space. Trapped in the cabin by Clark or another one of Tommy's men held no appeal. Those guys could be ruthless. They'd learned from evil itself.

After examining every crevice possible in the bathroom, she slowly spun in a circle, mulling over where Michael would have hidden the evidence she'd given him. Her gaze landed on the toilet. No way. She'd watched too many crime dramas. But yet… Tabitha lifted the tank lid, placed it on the seat, and peered in. "Bingo!"

"You found it?" Doug called from the other room.

"I think so." She reached in and pulled a baggie from the water. She held it over the tank and grabbed the hand towel from the bar to wipe her arm.

Doug stood in the doorway, hands braced on the frame. "Well?"

She lifted it to eye level. "One flash drive. It appears the plastic bag did its job." Tabitha handed it to Doug and replaced the lid.

He accepted the towel she gave him and dried the bag then stuffed the flash drive in his pocket. "I'd love to get a few hours of sleep, but I don't want to stay longer than necessary. I don't trust that Wade won't find this place. Time to leave before—"

An alarm blared in the cabin.

"What's that?" Tabitha's body shook from the jolt of the ear-piercing siren.

"Someone broke the perimeter."

"They found us?" She prayed she was wrong.

"Either that or someone just happened upon the cabin. Which isn't likely. Come on, let's check the monitor." Doug clasped her hand and tugged her down the hall toward the kitchen.

A gunshot, followed by an explosion of glass, sliced through the air.

"Doug?" Her hands trembled as she gripped the front of Doug's shirt.

Another crash of shattered glass. Gas fumes and smoke filled the small cabin.

"What are we going to do?" Flames danced in the living room a few feet high and continued to grow, blocking the entrance to the cabin.

He pointed to the small discs on the ceiling. "The sprinkler system will kick on and take care of the fire. But we have to get out of here."

"He'll see us if we leave through the back door. It's a long way to the trees."

"He won't see us." Doug grabbed her hand and tugged her into a hall closet.

She pulled against him. Tabitha didn't care if he had sprinklers or not. She refused to get into that small space. "We'll be trapped."

"I promise I'll get you out of here." The door flung open, revealing stairs that headed underground. He retrieved a backpack from a hook and slung it over his shoulder. "Stay close."

Not what she expected. Tabitha squinted into the dark area. What choice did she have? Face Tommy's goons or follow Doug? She prayed he knew what he was doing and wasn't signing their death certificate.

SIX

Thursday, 10:00 p.m.

The deceptive closet door closed behind them. Doug slid the bolt lock into place and guided Beth down the dark steps. He'd turn on the light but had no desire to telegraph their escape. In all the years he'd owned the cabin, not once had he envisioned using the underground escape. He'd bought the place from retired FBI Agent Willis Bankman, who'd used the cabin as a safe house. The man had built the extra security measures for high-profile clients. Right now, Doug could hug the guy for his paranoia that led to the addition.

"Shh. Stay quiet. We don't want whoever threw the Molotov cocktail through the window to find us," he whispered.

She squeezed his hand, which he interpreted as an acknowledgment of his request. Her trembling fingers sent a dagger through his heart, but he had no time to reassure her. He concentrated on each step away from the person trying to kill

Beth. His mind spun with the thought. Kill—not kidnap. Unless the person had gotten desperate and the fire was only a means to an end to flush her from the cabin.

The soft glow of a dim security light from the underground room guided Doug down the final few stairs. For the first time since his initial bout of overwhelming guilt over his wife's death, Doug rejoiced in the fact he'd allowed himself to indulge those feelings of insecurity. The lack of control of that situation had sent him over the edge. So, he'd taken his plans for the cabin over the top. The security system, the sprinkler system, and he'd maintained Agent Bankman's secret bedroom and escape route. Deep down, he knew he couldn't control everything in his life, but little things like that helped him cope with that reality.

He pulled Beth into the bedroom, closed the secondary door, and locked it.

"What is this place?" He had to strain to hear Beth's quiet question.

"A safety net." The stale odor from lack of use tickled his nose.

"But we're stuck! And the fire!" she whispered through gritted teeth. Doug thought Kyle's fiancée had that ability perfected, but Beth's skills rivaled Cassidy's.

He cleared his throat to cover his amusement.

He figured Beth wouldn't appreciate his laughter. Besides, he had to get Beth away from whoever remained outside. "The sprinkler system will take care of the fire. As for being stuck... the cabin has an escape route."

Now that his eyes had adjusted to the darkness, the tiny windows near the ceiling let in enough moonlight for him to see her owlish wide eyes. From the outside, the design simulated vents at the foundation of the cabin. No one would know it housed the equivalent of a safe room. "Let's just say I'm happy the man I bought this place from went overboard with the safety factor."

"Me too." She held his hand tight, cutting off his circulation, as he led her to the far wall.

"Stay right here." He released her and strode to the opposite side of the room. A couple packs of water bottles and hiking snacks were beneath the bed. He'd used the place for storage of nonperishable items. A few moments later, with the backpack filled with necessities, he rejoined Beth.

He led her into the closet and flipped a switch. A solid metal door opened to a long tunnel. "Follow me." Once she stepped through the entrance, he secured the door closed and continued along the underground path.

"Where does this exit?" Beth's whispers echoed off the walls.

Oh, this will go over great. "The outhouse."

She pulled him to a stop. "Say what?"

Doug chuckled. "Relax. It looks like an outhouse, but it's locked from the inside. I promise it's only a façade." He tugged her hand. "Come on."

At the end of the passage, Doug climbed the ladder and lifted the hatch. Once in the small room that appeared to be an old-fashioned outhouse from the exterior, he helped Beth climb up next to him. He lowered the access flap and scooted to the door. "Don't move."

The weight of the Glock against his palm loosened the knot that had formed between his shoulder blades. He edged to the door and peeked through the moon cutout that made the structure appear authentic. With the well-placed shrubs, he and Beth had a straight shot into the woods at the rear of the property. Agent Bankman was definitely getting a Christmas present this year. Assuming Doug and Beth made it out alive.

After one final scan for the person who'd attempted to kill them or, at minimum, tried to smoke them out, he slid the lock open. "The darkness will be good and bad. It'll be easier to go unnoticed, but picking our way through the woods will be difficult. Stay low and follow close."

"Lead the way," Beth whispered.

Doug eased the door open, examining the area

before slipping from the structure. Hunched low, he hurried toward the thick trees.

Beth kept pace behind him. The woods within reaching distance, she tripped and landed on her hands and knees with an "oof." The dried branches crunched beneath her, and a small branch snapped, signaling their location.

A gunshot ricocheted off the tree next to Doug. The bark splintered and tagged his neck. He lifted his weapon and returned fire. The person had fired blindly into the night. Otherwise, one or both of them would be dead.

"Hurry!" No longer worried about stealth mode, he grabbed Beth by the waist and half helped her run and half dragged her into the woods. "No time to stop. We have to get out of here."

Feet under her, she matched his stride. "I'm good. Go!"

Doug released his grip and took off through the overgrown brush. Blood trickled down his neck from the shower of bark, a cut he'd attend to when they found a place to hide for the night. The moonlight seeping through the trees gave little to no help. He picked his way through the darkness. Footfalls echoed behind them. Whoever had found his cabin refused to give up.

The whole situation gave him a mental pause. Two attempts at kidnapping. One break-in, obviously looking for something. And now the intent to kill, or so he assumed by the person's actions. Holding his Glock by his side, he continued through the brush. He lifted his left arm too late. A branch raked across his forearm and slapped him on the cheek. He hissed at the sting of the slash across his skin and chastised himself for losing focus.

A quick right turn took him and Beth deeper into the woods. If they'd continued in the original direction, they'd have ended up at the river. Which was where he planned to take her. But not until morning and the sun came up so he could see.

After what had felt like hours, Doug slowed and held his finger to his lips. He prayed they'd lost the person chasing them. Continuing in the dark was not an option. One or both of them would end up with a broken ankle or leg.

Beth nodded her understanding.

He tilted his head and listened for the person hunting them. When no movement met his ear, he motioned for Beth to follow. Certain the person who'd attacked wouldn't give up, he couldn't double back to the truck. Hiking to the river and following it to the next town seemed the only option. Maybe he'd borrow his closest neighbor's boat. But even that was a ways away.

The lack of light, coupled with the exhaustion

and aches from the day's events, made it impossible to keep going. He had to find a place to lie low for the night. With the aid of the moonlight peeking through the trees, Doug ducked between two large boulders and tucked into the farthest corner out of sight. He kicked his foot over the pine needles and leaves, chasing away unwanted critters. Snuggling up with something that slithered had no appeal to him. He shivered at the thought. Yes, he was man enough to admit that he'd scream like a two-year-old if that happened.

Doug lowered to the ground, praying nature wouldn't surprise him. He gently tugged Beth's hand and lowered his voice. "Have a seat."

She sat, leaned in, and found his ear. "Are we safe?"

Staying as quiet as possible, he whispered, "As long as whoever is chasing us doesn't look directly in here, we should be."

He felt the sag of her shoulders against his. "What now?"

"We get some rest." Thankful for a tiny bit of light from the night sky, he unzipped the backpack and pulled out two water bottles and a couple of protein bars. "It's not much, but at least we won't go hungry or thirsty."

She accepted the items. After unscrewing the cap on the water, she drank half then replaced the lid. She tapped on the pack and pretended to peek in. "What else do you have in that Mary Poppins bag?"

He snickered. "Several more waters and protein bars, a light jacket, waterproof matches, a small first aid kit, and a utility knife." Last year, he'd left the backpack holding the basics in the closet for those times he went hiking. He'd never expected to use it for survival.

With a long, slow exhale, Beth relaxed and nibbled on her food. "Thank you."

"For what?"

"Putting up with me." She shrugged. A sliver of moonlight touched her blonde hair.

"Believe me, it's not a hardship." In fact, it was anything but that. Once they finished drinking and eating, he collected the trash and shoved it into the bag. He retrieved the first aid kit. "I have a few cuts and scrapes that need to be cared for, and I'm sure you do too. Let's get those cleaned and bandaged before we rest."

"That sounds like a good idea."

Together they worked in tandem to treat each other's injuries. The lack of light made it difficult, but they took care of business in record time.

"Any other wounds?"

"No, I think we got them all. Thanks." A shiver shook Beth's body.

Doug snapped the kit shut, put it away, and retrieved the jacket from his backpack. "Come here." He draped the jacket over her, then wrapped an arm around her shoulders and drew her next to him. "Better?" A smile curved his lips when she snuggled into his side.

"Much."

A long night loomed for her to sleep upright, but it was all he could do. "Go ahead, get some rest. I'll keep watch." He removed his Glock from his holster and placed it in his lap, barrel pointed away from Beth.

The nocturnal sounds kept him on edge. The symphony of cicadas usually eased his tension, but on this particular night, the cacophony of buzzing tapped his brain like an ice pick. He strained his ears beyond the whining. Since the wildlife continued their normal activity, it told him no humans had come near. Pushing the ear-splitting noise aside, he closed his eyes and prayed. For wisdom. For safety. And for Beth.

Dawn began to make its presence known. Doug stifled a yawn and let the crisp morning air fill his lungs. He'd dozed on and off throughout the night, allowing his body to recover from the beating it had taken from the explosion and accident. He required more time to heal, but his aches and pains would have to wait until he got Beth to safety.

She shifted in his arms and peered up at him. "Good morning."

"Morning." His voice had deepened an octave in the early hours. He couldn't help but smile at her sleepy words. "It's time to eat breakfast and make a plan."

She stretched and winced.

"Take it easy. You're bound to be a bit sore today."

"That's an understatement." Beth folded the jacket she'd used for a blanket and handed it to him. "Thanks for the loan. I can't believe how chilly it got last night."

"Once the sun goes down, the temps tend to drop. Not enough for concern, just to be uncomfortable." He stuffed the jacket into the pack and removed another water bottle and protein bar. "Eat up. We'll need the fuel if we are going to hike out of here."

"We're not going back to the cabin?"

He shook his head. "My gut says that whoever is after you will be waiting for us."

Her brows pinched together. "You're probably right."

Now that she'd shed the cover and night gave way to day, Doug got a good look at her injuries. Scratches and shallow cuts marred her arms and legs. And she had a small gash on her cheek he assumed came from the branches. He chewed on his breakfast and made a mental note to keep an eye on the cut so it didn't get infected.

"What's up with the underground room and tunnel? Not that I'm complaining." Beth took a bite of her protein bar.

He scratched the stubble on his jaw. What he wouldn't give for a razor right now. Beards had never been his thing. He mulled over his answer. Not to hide the truth, but he preferred to collect his thoughts first. "Call it paranoia or an obsession. My anxiety hit an all-time high during that first week or so after Christine died. I'd failed her in the worst possible way, and I vowed never to let it happen to anyone I cared about ever again. So, I kept the secret room that Agent Bankman had created. I eventually intended to block off the tunnel and use it as a storage room or extra bedroom."

"I'm glad you kept it as is."

"Me too." His stomach roiled. What would have happened if he'd sealed off the escape route?

A shy smile graced her face. "Does your house in Valley Springs have the super spy room built in?"

His body shook with laughter, but he stayed quiet, unsure if the assailant lurked nearby. "No. Just a really awesome security system. The spy room, as you call it, was all on Agent Bankman." He tilted his head to listen for their attacker but heard nothing. He enjoyed talking with Beth but refused to ignore the threat.

Beth placed her hand on his and clutched his fingers.

The warmth of her touch eased the tension flowing through him. Once again, he recognized strength beneath her mousy exterior. The strong desire to persuade the courageous woman deep inside her to come out surprised him. "I told my therapist what I had bought and my plans. She encouraged me to preserve the escape route and continue with my security design. It gave me a sense of control when my world had shattered. It was rather cathartic. Between the physical labor and my sessions with my therapist, I began to slough off the guilt and found a bit of peace."

"Is it gone? Your guilt?" Beth's timidity returned.

"I still have my moments. Those events shaped who I've become—for better and worse." Doug studied her. Beth's injuries bothered him, but the night's rest had removed the dark circles under her eyes. He stowed the wrappers and the bottles in his pack and zipped the bag. "We need to keep moving. It's a long hike to the nearest town."

She combed her hair with her fingers and used the hair tie on her wrist to pull the strands into a ponytail. "How far?"

"By foot through the woods… I'd say four or five hours. It's not an easy trek through the forest. But we might be able to cut off a couple of hours. The river isn't far. My 'neighbor,' if you can call Wayne that since he lives so far away, has a fishing dock and a boat we might be able to borrow." Doug had never regretted the secluded location of his cabin until now.

"I wouldn't complain about that."

As if the woman had complained about anything. He holstered his Glock, slipped the backpack onto his shoulders, and adjusted the straps. "Ready?"

She nodded.

"Remember. Stay as quiet as possible." Doug rose and scanned the woods. Satisfied the person after them wasn't lurking in the trees, he helped Beth to her feet. "Let's go."

Doug picked his way through the bushes and brambles, attempting to find the clearest path possible. He hated the thought of inflicting more scrapes and bruises on Beth. As he moved toward the river, he prayed the assailant had given up but knew more than likely that wasn't the case. The first couple of attempts to take Beth had resulted in the attacker fleeing. This time, the person hadn't stopped to regroup. Something that bothered him more than he cared to admit.

But the information he and Beth retrieved was too important not to consider all the possibilities. He tapped his pocket, confirming the flash drive remained safe. If only his cell phone worked out here in the middle of nowhere. At the cabin, he had Wi-Fi, so communication with the outside world wasn't an issue. But in the forest… Maybe he should invest in a satellite phone to keep in the cabin. He shook his head and sighed. Now he was paranoid. Letting the differences between the attacks simmer in his mind, he continued the trek toward the river and prayed he didn't walk them into a trap.

Avoiding twigs and brambles was next to impossible. For the past hour, Tabitha had focused on the thick brush that twisted and tangled together on the ground. Doug had steered her down the most accessible paths possible, but she'd narrowly missed another branch to the face on more than one occasion. An outdoors girl she was not. But she refused to complain. It didn't help, and more times than not, it caused her pain. She'd learned that lesson early in life. Although the man who'd saved her life hadn't given her a reason to worry. However, old habits stuck like superglue. And she refused to push his patience.

Doug glanced over his shoulder. "Doing okay?" They'd quit whispering but continued to keep their voices low.

"As good as can be expected." What else could she say? The scratches on her arms and legs from the brush and insect bites stung, and her muscles ached. The accident hadn't done her any favors, but the hiking—that was another story.

He shoved another branch out of the way. "Do you need to stop?"

Did she? Um, that would be a yes. Would she admit it? No. "I can keep going." Her stomach chose that moment to gurgle. *No, not now.* She'd passed the morning sickness stage, but the lack of food in her belly hadn't helped. The protein bar she'd eaten a little while ago had disappeared from her system, leaving her stomach to gnaw on itself. She placed a hand on her belly and willed the nausea to go away.

"Hey, what's wrong?"

She glanced up in time to avoid running into Doug's broad chest. Her gaze met his. In her entire life, she'd never had a man look at her with the concern or compassion that filled his brown eyes. Her mouth worked before her brain engaged. "I'm a bit tired, that's all."

Hands on her shoulders, he dipped his chin and peered at her. "Then we should rest for a minute."

The intensity in his gaze threw her off-balance. She cleared her throat. "Yeah, that might be a good idea."

His eyes drifted to her lips and back up. After a moment, he nodded. "I spotted a log just ahead. It'll make for a good place to sit."

Her heart rate spiked. Had he wanted to kiss

her? More importantly, would she have let him? Ugh. Why had she allowed her mind to go there? She shoved the thought away and focused on keeping the contents, or lack thereof, of her stomach where it belonged.

Doug brushed the pine needles and leaves from the log and patted the space next to him. "Have a seat before you fall down." He placed the backpack between his feet and retrieved a water bottle.

She joined him and accepted the drink. "Thanks."

"I have a few pieces of candy in here." He dug in the pack, found the sweet treat, and handed it to her. "Peppermint. It'll help settle your stomach and give your blood sugar a boost. Once that's under control, I'll give you another protein bar."

"Wait. How did you know?" Her heart rate shot up. Had he figured out her secret?

"You look a little green." He shrugged. "Just put two and two together."

She swallowed the panic crawling up her throat. Had his math added up to knowing she was pregnant? Oh, how she hoped not. She accepted the candy and popped it in her mouth. The sweetness melted on her tongue. The peppermint flavor quickly eased the churning in her belly. She sat in silence as the sugar infiltrated through her system.

He broke a protein bar in half and handed it to her. "I don't want you to overdo it. Eat half, and once that settles, you can finish the rest of it a little later."

She nibbled on the offered food. Between the sugar and the protein, the nausea disappeared.

Doug shifted on the log to face her and tucked a strand of flyaway hair behind her ear. "Better?"

"Much." She ducked her head, hiding her tears. The more she tried to avoid feelings for the handsome detective, the more he burrowed his way into her heart. Birds chirped above, and a slight breeze rustled the trees. The peaceful surroundings gave her a false sense of security. "Do you think he's still out there?"

"Yes." Doug sighed. "I'll be honest with you. I'm praying he gave up and returned to the cabin. But my gut tells me he won't walk away. I'm guessing Kyle's truck is still intact, and the guy didn't eliminate our transportation out of here. But when he threw the Molotov cocktail to smoke us from the cabin, as far as I'm concerned, he took away that possibility. Whoever this guy is, he's determined. He probably hoped we'd try for the vehicle as an escape plan, but I'm not comfortable doubling back. We've only seen one person, but I'm banking on him having backup."

Doug's little rundown of the facts sent a shiver snaking up her spine. "Then let's get that flash drive into the hands of your friends." Eyes closed, she inhaled. She could do this—had to do this—if she wanted freedom from Tommy.

Doug readjusted the backpack and helped her to her feet. "It's about another thirty-minute hike to the river, then we'll follow it a little ways and hope we find Wayne's boat." He clenched his teeth, tightening the muscles in his jaw.

"Doug?" She swung her gaze from one side to the other, searching for what had caused his reaction.

"Sorry. Just thinking." He jerked his head, indicating for her to follow him on their trek through the woods. "If I were the one hunting us, the river is where I'd make my stand. It makes the most sense."

Her stomach dropped. "So, we're walking into a trap?"

He scratched the back of his head as he kept walking. "Maybe."

Beth wanted to run screaming in the other direction, but Doug had protected her so far. She knew deep down that he'd do everything in his power to keep her safe. She hoped it was enough.

SEVEN

Friday, 10:00 a.m.

The stress of yesterday, that's what had made Doug lose his mind. It had to be. What other excuse did he have? He'd come seconds from kissing Beth before breaking the connection that seemed to tether them. From what she'd told him, men had manipulated and used her all her life. She was scared and on the run. He refused to be another person who took advantage of her vulnerability. But he couldn't deny the pull of attraction. Beth's hidden strength had latched on to him, and he wasn't sure what to do about it. And that right there—his uncertainty—the reason he wouldn't allow himself the privilege of kissing her.

With the sun filtering through the trees, the warmth and humidity had risen from the dip in temperatures of last night. Sweat trickled between his shoulder blades from the pack resting against his back. His boots crunched on the dry undergrowth. The attacker hadn't shown himself, but Doug's neck hair prickled with awareness of someone close—a sixth sense he'd developed overseas, and he'd learned not to ignore it.

A twig snapped to his left. He halted, causing Beth to run into him. "Be very quiet." He mouthed. Then snatched his Glock from the holster on his waistband and put a finger to his lips.

She nodded and remained still.

He scanned the area and came up empty. However, he didn't trust his sight. He trusted his instincts. A small section of fallen trees caught his attention. Hand on Beth's arm, he gently led her to the spot. "Tuck in there and don't make a sound," he whispered.

After a quick nod, she hurried to the nest made of fallen trees and wiggled in. He handed her the backpack. She'd need the water and food in case he wasn't able to return as soon as he planned. The trust in her eyes when she peered up at him through the limbs gutted him. His doubts came raging back, but he refused to let them take hold. Beth was too precious for him to fail.

Pulling on his experiences, he switched mindsets from the hunted to the hunter. He moved away from Beth, hoping to draw the person insistent on hurting her in the opposite direction. Alone in the woods, he stepped with care, avoiding leaving tracks. At least as few as possible.

Doug circled around, coming at the person trailing them from behind—he hoped. Movement flashed in the corner of his eye. The person headed toward Beth's hiding spot. His heart pounded, threatening to explode from his chest. Doug switched directions. He had to lead the attacker away from her.

A new plan formed in his mind. He searched the ground, found the perfect thin limb, and stepped on it. The twig snapped, scattering the birds in the trees surrounding him. He faded into the background and waited.

An unidentifiable figure appeared. The person's stealth movement screamed of training. Military—maybe. Either way, Doug's concern quadrupled. He'd have to up his game several levels to get Beth out of the woods alive.

He ducked out of sight and leaned against a tree trunk. He took a minute to regulate his breathing, then continued with his plan of leading the guy away from Beth.

Forty minutes later, covered in sweat and sure he'd lost the person, Doug returned to where he'd left her.

He picked through the brush and found the log nest with her nestled inside. "Beth?"

"I'm here." A small voice came from the hole. Her gaze met his. She dug in the pack and produced a water bottle. "Drink. You look like you need it."

"Thanks." He slid his Glock into the holster at his hip, accepted the bottle, and downed the entire thing. "I lost him—for the moment. Let's take advantage of it." He helped her to her feet, and the two continued toward his objective—the river.

Several minutes later, he slowed, allowing Beth to close the short distance between them. He estimated another forty-five minutes to the most dangerous section of the escape.

"Did you see something?" she whispered.

"We're getting close to the water. We'll be out in the open as we exit the woods and make our way to the river's edge. I might have temporarily lost the guy after us, but the river is a great place for an ambush."

"Thanks for that visual."

The snarky reply had Doug turning toward Beth. The smirk on her face brought a smile to his own. "There she is."

Beth's brows pinched together. "What?"

"That strong tiger beneath the surface." The privilege of witnessing Beth's transformation from a scared girl to a strong, tough woman wasn't lost on him.

She smacked his arm with the gentleness of a kitten. "I am not a tiger."

"You are in my eyes. You have more strength

than you realize. You're willing to sacrifice to take down one of the biggest and meanest drug dealers in the Midwest. I call that grit."

"One way or another, Tommy isn't getting away with his crimes this time." Sadness flashed in Beth's eyes and vanished as quickly as it had appeared. "But to address your comment, sometimes you don't have a choice."

"Whatever the reason, you are showing your claws and scratching your way out of your circumstances." Doug flipped her words on end and then upside down. Something about not having a choice struck him as important. She'd trusted him with her past, but he sensed more secrets she'd yet to reveal.

Beth scraped her teeth across her lower lip. "Maybe. We'll see what happens in the end."

He retrieved his Glock from the holster on his waistband. The person he'd led away from Beth had skills. Taking Beth out in the open had Doug on edge, but his choices were limited. He didn't have enough water or food to last much longer. Plus, Beth appeared ready to drop. The time had come to get her to civilization. "From here on out, we move with care. Be aware of your surroundings, and let me know if you feel something off."

She nodded, but fear flashed across her features.

"Before we move, answer me this... Would

Wade try to eliminate you, or would he try to take you back?" The question had taken root and bothered him since the explosion at the cabin.

Beth chewed on the inside of her cheek. A habit Doug wanted to break her of. "If he thinks I'll testify against him, he'll kill me, and my death wouldn't be quick. I'm not important to him other than a plaything he can possess. But his thing is control, so I'd say, first and foremost, he wants me back under his power."

"The kidnapping makes sense." Doug let her statement roll around in his brain. "But why try to kill you at the cabin or shoot at you when we ran into the woods? He'd want the evidence. The man wouldn't leave it out there for someone to accidently find."

Her head snapped up. "You're right. He'd *make* me tell him where it is. Not kill me without the information."

"Once we are out of this mess, that's an inconsistency that bears exploring." He set out toward their destination. Sweat slicked his palm gripping his gun. He shifted the Glock to his other hand, wiped the moisture on his pants, and returned his weapon to where it belonged. If you drew a straight line, his closest neighbor Wayne lived five miles away—if you could call that close through the thick of woods. He counted on the fishing boat being moored to the dock his neigh-

bor had told him about. He planned to borrow
said boat, head downriver to the next town and
call his team. Assuming they made it through the
last part of the journey alive.

The flow of water rose above the sounds of
life among the trees. He placed his back against
a trunk and pulled Beth beside him. "Stay here.
I'm going to have a look around."

"Be careful."

He slipped his hand into hers and squeezed,
hoping to reassure her. He leaned into her ear.
"Have a seat and stay really quiet." Not wanting
to leave her vulnerable but not having a choice,
he slipped away.

The low-hanging branches surrounding Beth
should conceal her position while he examined
the area. He hated leaving her, but once they left
the shelter of the woods, the vulnerability of at-
tack would increase drastically. An examination
of the area was a necessity.

He ducked under another tree limb and stepped
with a light foot through the woods, limiting his
tracks. His mind wandered to Beth. Was she
okay? Had the person slipped by him and found
her? His steps faltered. His heart had gotten involved. He couldn't deny it. Something about the
wounded woman grabbed him and refused to let
go.

As he circled around and headed back toward

Beth, a peculiar-shaped tuft of loose dirt next to a tree trunk caught his attention. Not a typical animal mark, but he wouldn't rule it out either. Doug knelt and examined the oddity. He narrowed his gaze. Disturbed leaves and twigs lay in unnatural angles. He brushed the dried foliage away, revealing the imprints of a person using the section by the tree as a resting point.

Whoever had tried to roast him and Beth alive had tracked them down. He had to return to Beth and get her out of these woods.

With a quick pace, he hurried back to Beth. He entered the dense shrubbery and peered toward the thick brush. His heart jackhammered against his breastbone. She wasn't there. "Beth!" he whisper-yelled.

"Right here."

He spun and saw two eyes peeking through the brush. He gulped in air, pushing down the fear that threatened to consume him. "What are you doing in there?"

She crawled out on her hands and knees, then reached back and retrieved the backpack. He helped her to her feet. "I heard a noise. It sounded like a person walking through the woods. I hid."

He ran his hand down her arm. "Okay. Good." Flashes of horrible images flipped through his mind and made his stomach churn. He couldn't lose another woman he cared about.

"Did you find anything?"

Doug scooped up the backpack and slipped it onto his back. "Yes. Our firebug is out there. Or at least I'm assuming it's the same person."

"You saw him?" Beth's eyes widened.

"No. But I found marks that someone tried very hard to conceal." He hated worrying her, but honesty would keep her alert and aware of her surroundings. "The best thing we can do is get to Wayne's and pray he didn't take his boat out fishing."

She chewed on her bottom lip. Tiny red spots dotted the soft skin.

He cupped her cheek. "Stop. You're making it bleed."

"Sorry." She dipped her head and lowered her gaze to the ground. "I won't do it again." The strong woman who'd emerged a little while ago disappeared.

"Beth, look at me." With a gentle nudge, he lifted her chin. The subservient gesture raised his anger at Tommy Wade and every man who'd treated her like dirt. When she refused to meet his eyes, he added a bit more pressure. "Please."

She swallowed hard and lifted her gaze.

"That's better." They had to move—soon. But he needed the tiger he'd witnessed earlier with him as they moved on. "Just know you don't ever have to apologize when you've done nothing wrong. I only wanted you to stop hurting yourself."

No words, but she gave him a quick nod. He'd take it.

"We'll walk inside the tree line for as long as possible to hide our progress, but there will be a point when we won't have cover. At that point, we'll be an open target, so move fast."

She inhaled and jutted her chin in determination. "Got it. Lead on."

And there she was. His tiger had returned. He withdrew his Glock and held it against his leg. "Stay close."

Sweat dripped from his temples. He slapped his neck, killing the mosquito that landed on his skin for a snack. He'd paused their trek several times for him and Beth to hydrate and snack on the last of his protein bars. They hadn't stopped for any length of time, only to fuel up. Her pallor worried him, but she'd waved off his concerns and muscled on.

The open stretch of land loomed ahead. Doug halted and scanned the most dangerous section of their escape. Nothing seemed out of place. But experience told him not to let his guard down.

"I'm going to see if the boat is there. Stay out of sight. I'll be back soon." He waited until Beth ducked into the brush, strode along the edge of the woods, and found the dock Wayne had described. He exhaled with relief. A silver fishing boat with a motor bobbed on the water. Their way out, only feet away. Time to retrieve Beth and get out of Dodge.

With silent strides, he reached where he'd left her. "Ready to go?"

She shrieked. Birds flapped and scattered from the limbs above. Her hand flew to her mouth. "I'm so sorry."

"My fault. I'll be more careful not to startle you next time." He kept his voice calm as his gaze roamed the shoreline, all the while praying her reaction hadn't summoned the person chasing her. Not convinced they'd avoided the attacker but in a hurry to get Beth out of there after the noise, he pointed downstream. "The boat is just over there. Let's get out of here."

Tears flooded her eyes, and her hand covered her stomach. "Yes, please."

"Once we get in the boat, lay on the bottom until we put some distance between us and this part of the forest." He clutched her fingers.

"Anything you say." Her hand trembled in his.

The thirty feet of open space between the tree line and the boat felt like a mile. He shifted his gun to his left hand—not ideal, but he was proficient with his nondominant hand—then tucked her into his right side. "Straight to the boat. No matter what you see or hear, you get in and duck down. I'll start the engine and get us out of here."

"I promise."

Doug took several deep breaths. He hadn't seen or heard the person after Beth, but the hairs on his nape prickled. "Come on." He hurried to the dock. Beth kept pace and stayed glued to his side. Their shoes clomped on the long strip of boards.

He kneeled and pulled the boat toward him by the rope that tethered the vessel to the old wooden planks. One foot in the boat and one on the dock, he extended a hand to help her aboard. He sent up a silent prayer of thanks they'd made it that far without incident.

Beth stepped into the vessel. It rocked with the shift of weight, and she grabbed his arm to steady herself.

Doug widened his stance, allowing her time to regain her balance. "Got it?"

"Yes, thank you." Beth released her tight grip.

A shot exploded through the air.

Fire tore through his left arm. The force of the bullet spun him and slammed his head against the gunwale before dropping him to the deck. His weapon skidded along the bottom of the boat.

Beth's scream pierced the foggy haze taking over his head.

White light flashed behind his eyelids. The pain—intense. The excruciating agony, the only reason he knew his arm remained attached. He sucked in air through his clenched teeth, fighting against the pain and the nausea roiling in his belly. He had to get Beth away from the shooter.

"Doug!" Beth scrambled to his side.

"Get down!" He pushed her beneath the gunwale. Risking exposure, he flipped the line off the cleat that held the boat to the dock.

Swallowing the bile that rose in his throat, he crawled toward the wheel. Ignoring the pain was next to impossible as he struggled to get them away from the shooter. The key sticking out from the ignition almost made him cry like a baby. His fingers fumbled with the key and prayed the engine started on the first try. He practically collapsed in relief when the boat hummed to life.

Another bullet pinged off the rail.

He ducked below the wheel and eased the throttle forward, turning the boat to the left. The long dock out into the water gave him room to maneuver the vessel. After he managed to point the boat downriver, he pushed the throttle forward and put distance between them and the gunman.

Once he felt safe, he hefted into the seat and slowed the vessel. He swayed and gripped the wheel tighter to keep himself upright.

He took the speed down another notch, worried that in his agony-filled state, he'd steer them into the bank. "Beth?"

"I'm right here." Her hand clutched his right shoulder.

He rolled his head to the side, cautious not to trigger dizziness, and caught his first glimpse at her arm. Blood dribbled to her elbow and dripped onto the deck. "You're hurt."

She glanced at her injury and shrugged. "I'm fine. You, on the other hand…"

Yeah, his head hurt from hitting the edge of the boat, but the hot poker sensation in his arm had dissipated. Come to think of it, his limb had gone numb. "I…um…" The world blurred and tilted.

He blinked away the dark cloud. The engine sat idle as the boat bobbed on the water. Doug realized a bit late that Beth had removed the pack from his back and found the small first aid kit he kept for emergencies.

"Welcome back. I have to stop the bleeding, or at least slow it down."

His gaze drifted down to find her wrapping his wound in gauze. Black dots danced along the edge of his vision.

"Stay with me. Don't fall asleep. You're too big for me to move without help." She finished and maneuvered behind him. "On three, you're going to do your best to swing from the captain's seat to the cushion I've placed over at the side."

He glanced to his right and sighed. Oh, yeah, he was going to lose his lunch if he moved. But he'd be the first to admit the adrenaline had faded, and his injury had made him a liability, not an asset. "Got it."

Beth counted down, and somehow, he made it to the makeshift seat without hurling. He rested his head against the side of the boat, closed his eyes, and willed the throbbing to go away.

A warm hand cupped his cheek. "Are you still with me?"

"Yeah." Just barely. He peeked through the tiny slits of his eyelids. The energy required to keep his eyes open was beyond belief. He inhaled in hopes of clearing the cobwebs from his brain.

The engine hummed once again, and the boat continued down the river. Beth had taken over without a complaint. Yup, his mouse had the heart of a tiger. The corner of his mouth lifted. Or at least he thought it had.

"Doug?"

"I'm here." Although sleep tugged at him, he maintained a semi-coherent status. It would be so easy to allow it to pull him under.

"Tell me about your wife." Beth's voice rose over the engine.

He lifted an eyelid. "Why?"

She stood tall, but her white-knuckle grip on the wheel belied her at-ease appearance. "I'd like to know. And I need you to keep talking so you stay conscious."

He snorted. "That's one way to do it." Doug let his mind drift to the past. "Christine was tenacious. With me being in the Army and deployed for long periods of time, she had to be. I was young and stupid. Not easy to live with. But that didn't stop her." He chuckled and groaned. Mental note to self, don't laugh. "She was the CEO of a security firm. That's how we met. A friend of a friend introduced us. We had a passion for cybersecurity in common and hit it off."

"Wow, CEO. She did well for herself then."

"She did. Let's just say that I'm not hurting in the money department because of her success." He shifted to ease the pressure on his back. "Don't get me wrong. I still have to work, but I don't have to worry about finances."

Beth bobbed her head up and down, signaling her understanding. "I'm sorry you lost her."

"Yeah, me too. But life continues, and Christine is a happy memory for me now." Except... did he open up and tell her? Why not? What did he have to lose? Everything, that's what, but his brain wasn't firing on all cylinders. He knew it, but his mouth had a mind of its own. "One of my biggest regrets."

Her gaze scanned the edges of the river before refocusing on the waterway in front of them. "What's that?"

"I've only told one other person. My boss, Dennis."

"Your secret is safe with me." She flashed him a smile.

He closed his eyes and let the memory flood his mind. "I have a hard time letting go of my guilt, not only because my wife was murdered in our home, and I wasn't there to save her. But because she was pregnant. I not only failed my wife, but my unborn son."

Beth's harsh intake of breath hissed over the background noise.

"It's hard to ignore that little detail when people tell me there was nothing I could do from thousands of miles away." At her silence, Doug forced his eyes open.

Beth sat ramrod straight. Tears poured down her cheeks.

"Beth, what's wrong?"

She shook her head.

Nausea returned with a vengeance. Not because of his wounds. Did Beth blame him for his wife and unborn son's death?

Tabitha steered the boat down the middle of the river. A loose strand of hair whipped across her face. Tears stuck a wayward piece to her cheek. She hooked it with a finger and tucked it behind her ear. Her arm chose that moment to remind her of the bullet that went straight through Doug's arm and sliced across hers. The gash burned, and blood soaked her sleeve. At least the bleeding had appeared to stop. Unlike her brain that continued to process Doug's words.

Her stomach flopped. Pregnant? The little confidence Beth had mustered since Doug rescued her disintegrated. The man had admitted to a fear of failure with his wife and son. Would he continue to help Tabitha if he knew about her unborn baby? Could he risk his fear of failure and be responsible for another woman and unborn baby? A shiver raced up her spine, even with the rising temperatures and sun shining overhead. And what about her growing feelings for him?

"Beth?"

"Yeah?" She refused to look at him. The man was as perceptive as they came.

"I asked what was wrong."

"Nothing. You just caught me by surprise." Her hand brushed over her belly. She would face any evil head-on for the tiny life inside.

"I know I failed in a big way back then, but I promise I'll do my best to protect you."

She went against her vow not to look him in the eye and glanced in his direction. "I know you will." And that was the problem. He'd help her until he found out about the baby. Then he'd realize that protecting her wasn't worth the emotional anguish of protecting another unborn baby.

He pulled his cell phone from his back pocket and winced. His face paled, and his breathing came in pants.

The pained response stabbed her in the heart. The man had already sacrificed so much for her. She slowed the boat and shifted her gaze to him. "Try not to move."

He swallowed, and his Adam's apple bobbed. "Waiting for cell service to call for help."

"That's a good idea since I have no idea where I'm going." She'd said more than a few prayers for Doug to stay conscious and guide her to safety.

"You're doing great. I'm sorry I'm not any help. But if I move, I'll puke."

"Please do not move then." She didn't do well with vomit, especially now. She cringed even thinking about it.

Doug palmed his phone and rested his head against the side of the boat. "No service yet."

"Do you think the shooter followed us?" Tabitha scanned the woods on either side of the river.

"I don't see how. We took the only boat. My guess is he went back to the cabin."

The rustle of leaves and birds singing in trees filled the silence that lingered between them.

Tabitha kept the boat pointed down the middle of the river. She glanced at the man who'd promised to protect her. His closed eyes and taut mouth worried her. "Doug, are you awake?"

"Yeah." He blinked and focused on her.

"We can't stay on the water forever. Where am I going?"

He tilted his head forward and examined their surroundings. "In a little bit, you'll see a marina to your right. Pull into any slip you see vacant." He checked his phone. A heavy release of breath escaped. "We have cell service."

A weight lifted from her shoulders. She'd stretched her abilities when Doug had all but collapsed. "Thank you, Jesus."

"Amen to that." Doug hit speed dial and lifted the phone to his ear. "Kyle…if you'd stop talking, I'd tell you…" He rolled his eyes. "Fine… I need backup at Cooper's Marina."

"And send an ambulance!" She hoped Kyle heard her request.

Doug's chin dropped to his chest. "Yes, an ambulance would be appreciated…through and through in my upper arm, and I hit my head… no, I don't think it's serious…she's okay, but the bullet went through me before it sliced across her arm. She'll probably need stitches…got it. Thanks." Doug hung up. "Kyle's on his way. He checked the GPS tracker on my phone. Said we are about three miles from the marina."

The relief hit Tabitha hard. Her hands shook on the wheel, and her knees almost buckled.

Ten minutes later, she steered toward the dock. She had no idea how to park a boat. Was that what people called it? "Um, Doug? I'm not sure how to do this."

He pushed to his feet and hunched over, holding onto the rail. A low groan fell from his lips. "Slow down and ease next to the dock." He staggered but steadied himself before he fell.

Panic clawed at her. What if she messed up? What if she hurt the boat? Doug had never yelled at her or lifted a hand against her. But that's not to say he wouldn't. She took a deep breath, stuffed the fears aside, and focused on the task of getting them safely to the dock.

"That's it. You're doing great." Doug's sluggish words, the encouragement she needed.

She bumped the boat against the dock and whimpered. Her gaze popped to Doug.

He stumbled, then righted himself. He grabbed the rope to tie off the boat. It took two tries before he looped it around the metal cleat. A moment later, he turned and slid to a seated position. "Shut it down. We'll wait for Kyle to finish securing the boat."

She questioned turning off the engine. They'd be stuck without a quick escape if her attacker found them before Doug's partner arrived. She scanned the area one last time, then flipped the key to the off position. The hum of the engine ceased. "How long until he gets here?"

As if on cue, sirens wailed in the distance.

Knowing help would arrive soon, Tabitha shoved aside her reservations and knelt beside Doug. She clasped the hand on his good arm. "How can I help?"

A smile tugged at the corner of his mouth. "You're doing it." He released her and held out his arm. "Come here."

She hesitated. Her concerns about how he would react to her baby continued to linger. But in the end, she accepted his offer and snuggled into his side. His warmth, a cocoon around her. Even with all her doubts and fears, for the first time in Tabitha's life, hope of a life without dread bloomed within. "Thank you."

Doug kissed the top of her head. "I should be thanking you for saving us. You were amazing."

Boots clomped on the wooden dock, and several voices floated in the air. Tabitha lifted her gaze. Kyle sprinted toward them with two male paramedics in his wake.

"Doug! Ta—Beth!" Kyle caught himself from using her real name before he outed her to the world—or at least the two men behind him. He got on his knees and pulled the edge of the boat closer. "Brent, grab the line and secure it to the dock."

"Got it. Ethan, hold on to the gurney." Brent ensured his partner had a grip on the bed they'd rolled down the dock, then assisted Kyle.

The boat rocked as Kyle stepped in. "Let's get you two out of here. And from the looks of the blood..." He pointed to Doug's arm and her sleeve. "To the hospital." Kyle offered her his hand.

She accepted his gesture and stepped onto the dock with the help of the paramedic Kyle had called Brent. Once steady on the wood planks, she moved to the side.

Brent stepped into the boat and grabbed the medical bag Ethan handed him. The man took Doug's blood pressure and pulse. After checking for a concussion with a penlight, Brent unwound the bandage she'd applied and assessed Doug's gunshot wound. Blood had stopped flowing from the hole and only trickled down Doug's arm. Brent cleaned it with a saline solution and re-wrapped the injured arm. "Think you can get out of this thing without falling flat on your face?"

The glare Doug sent the medic had Tabitha biting her lip to keep from laughing. The man was stubborn.

Brent shook his head. "Mule." Kyle flanked Doug's other side, and the two all but lifted him out. Ethan took over, slung Doug's good arm over his shoulders, and gripped him around the waist.

Within minutes, Brent and Ethan had Doug strapped to the gurney with an IV in place.

"Bring her to the ambulance." Ethan threw the command over his shoulder to Kyle.

Kyle cupped her elbow and escorted her to the parking lot. "You'll go with Doug to the hospital. I'll meet you there. Don't worry. I'll watch for a tail."

Not sure what else to do, she nodded. Kyle helped her up into the ambulance and onto the bench seat. Once settled, he hopped down and closed the doors. Two slaps on the medic unit later, signaling the truck was clear to go, Brent drove away.

"How's he doing?" she asked Ethan.

"He'll be fine. I gave him something for the pain, so he's a bit out of it." Ethan swung to the seat beside her. "Now that I know Doug is out of danger, let me see that arm of yours."

"It's just a scratch." She'd had worse in her life—much worse.

Ethan didn't comment, just scrunched her short sleeve above the gash and carefully twisted her arm to examine the wound. "A bit more than a scratch, but nothing a good cleaning and a few stitches won't fix."

Once at the hospital, the rear doors opened,

and Brent and Ethan hurried Doug into the emergency room, leaving a nice nurse named Terri to assist her from the ambulance.

"Watch your step." Terri grasped her hand as she eased her to the ground. "Let's get you inside and examine at that injury."

An hour later, alone in the emergency bay, Tabitha inhaled through her nose and exhaled through her mouth three times, forcing her anxiety into the background. She hated hospitals. Her entire life, men had coached her on what to say to doctors so as to not implicate those men in abusing her. Lying on the hospital bed, she toyed with the edge of the blanket and worried her lower lip. No one had told Tabitha about Doug's condition. Her mind spun all kinds of wild scenarios. Then again, she wasn't family, so why should they tell her anything. She barely qualified as a friend—if that.

The white curtain zipped open, and Tabitha flinched. Her heart rate spiked.

"Hi, Beth. Can I come in?" Detective Cassidy Bowman, Kyle's fiancée, stood by the curtain with a small bag in her hand.

"Sure." She slowed her breathing. Funny how Cassidy's presence gave her a boost of comfort.

"First things first. I know how things happen around hospitals. I practically lived in one for a while." She gestured to the burn scars on her arm, then waved her hand like swatting a fly. "But that's a story for another day. Doug is fine. Oh, he'll be sore, no doubt. But the bullet was a through and through. I guess you know that though, considering it took a slice out of your arm."

Tabitha tilted her head, amused at the whirlwind named Cassidy. When she'd met the detective, the woman appeared no-nonsense yet quiet. She hadn't seen the more energetic side of her.

"Anyhoo, they sedated Doug and are cleaning out the wound and stitching him up. He lost a lot of blood, but they don't have to do surgery, so that's good. His head is another story. Doc's concerned, but since Doug answered the man's questions coherently, he's reserving judgment until Doug can demonstrate balance. If he passes that, Doc will release him. He'll be sore and grumpy when the drugs wear off."

"So, it isn't serious?" She wanted to cry with relief for the man who'd vowed to protect her.

Cassidy shook her head. "Nope. He's got a hard head, so he should be fine on that front." The detective chuckled. "And as for the bullet, it hit the fleshy part of his arm. Maybe a bit of muscle, but nothing serious. I'm sure it won't take him long to annoy the physical therapist."

Tabitha sagged on the bed. "Good."

"Now, for the second thing." Cassidy held up the small bag. "A change of clothes for you."

"Oh, thank you." She pinched the front of her top and pulled. The ripe odor of sweat from traipsing through the woods had clung to her skin and seeped into the fabric. "Not only is this stained with blood, I'm sure it smells."

"Come on, I'll help you clean up, and then we can escape."

Tabitha rolled and swung her legs over the edge of the bed. "I want to see Doug."

"I figured you'd say that." The detective held out her hand. "Then let's get to it."

Tabitha accepted her assistance. "I appreciate you stopping by and letting me know about Doug. And for bringing me clothes."

"That's what friends do."

"I haven't had many of those. I'm not sure how to respond." For whatever reason, honesty poured from Tabitha. "I don't understand why you all have turned your lives upside down for me."

Cassidy squeezed her hand. "Bottom line… we care."

Tabitha relished the comfort and closeness. She still didn't understand completely, but she'd accept the kindness.

"We want to help. That's all. No hidden agenda." Cassidy cocked her head to the side. "Would it bother you to know that I'll be your shadow until Doug is up and functional again?"

She hadn't forgotten about Tommy and his

men, but the harsh reality slammed into her. She shook off the panic that threatened to take over. "Not at all. In fact, I welcome it."

"Dude, would you stop pacing? You're giving me a headache." Doug would beg if it'd convince Kyle to halt his path back and forth across the room.

The doctor had insisted that Doug stay overnight due to the IV of antibiotics and blood loss. The mild concussion hadn't helped his cause either. He'd begged to go home to recuperate, but Dennis had vetoed that plan. Doug hated the fuss but didn't have the energy to argue.

The nurses had transferred him to a private room twenty minutes ago. He hadn't seen Beth since the ambulance ride, but Kyle assured him she was safe and under Cassidy's watchful eye.

Doug shifted and groaned. "Remind me not to move."

Kyle paused by his bed and smirked. "Pssh. It's only a scratch."

That scratch, as Kyle called it, required a couple layers of stitching to close the hole that went through his arm. Doug glared at his partner. "Why are we friends again?"

"Because you love me like a brother."

"I'm rethinking that." The look of mock horror on Kyle's face made Doug laugh. He grabbed his elbow to support his slinged arm and groaned. "Please. Stop. It hurts."

The door swung open and whacked against the wall.

Doug tensed and scanned the room for a weapon as Kyle drew his Glock and leveled it on the visitor.

"Would you put that thing away before you hurt someone?" Miss Judith Evans, the town dynamo and the Anderson County Sheriff's Department's adopted grandmother, stood in the entry to the room with her hands on her hips, cane dangling from her fingers. Her perfectly formed eyebrow arched, and her full attention zeroed in on Kyle.

"Miss Judith, I could have shot you. Why didn't you knock?" Kyle grumbled.

"Young man, if you can't tell the difference between me and one of your unruly criminals, you don't deserve to wear that badge."

The woman was priceless. Doug slid his hand over his mouth to hide his chuckle.

Kyle sighed and holstered his Glock. "Come in and have a seat." His partner scooted a chair next to the bed.

Doug adored Miss Judith. The woman was wise beyond her years, and that was saying something since she was well into her eighties. "To what do I owe this visit? Not that I'm unhappy to see you. Quite the opposite."

"I see someone has some manners around here." Judith leveled her gaze on Kyle, shook her head, and tsked. She turned her attention to Doug and patted his arm without the bullet hole. "I was here visiting a friend when I heard the commotion. So, I hunted you down and came to see how my boy is doing."

If the world didn't know about his injury, they did now. Miss Judith wasn't known for being discreet. Especially if it involved her "boys." And since the women had come into the picture, Miss Judith had enveloped them into the special group.

"I've been better, but Doc patched me up. I'll be as good as new in no time."

"Scuttlebutt has it you're protecting our Beth." Classic Judith. The older woman claimed half the town as hers even without the connection to the sheriff's department.

He nodded. "I am—or was until this." He patted his elbow in the sling.

"Who's with the poor girl now?" Judith leveled another glare at Kyle.

"Good grief, Miss Judith." Kyle rolled his eyes. "She's with Cassidy. You know I have Doug's back."

"Just checking." Judith's attention returned to him. "How is that darling girl? Every time Harold and I visit the café, I worry about her. She seems nervous."

"Don't worry. She's safe." Doug pressed the control button and raised the bed's head a little more. He grimaced at the movement. Judith clutched his hand and squeezed. He dearly loved this woman. "So, has Harold popped the question yet?" The entire town waited for Judith's boyfriend to ask the woman to marry him. But so far, the two seemed happy to be just friends.

"Well, now that you've brought it up." Judith placed her left hand on Doug's forearm. A delicate diamond ring winked at him.

"Miss Judith! Why didn't you say anything?" Kyle scolded.

"Say anything about what?" Dennis waltzed in with Jason at his heels.

"Seems our Miss Judith has gone and gotten herself engaged." Doug grinned. "Since I can't come to you, lean down here so I can congratulate you properly." Judith obliged, and he placed a kiss on the woman's cheek.

Silence lingered after Judith dropped the engagement bomb. Then one by one, the other men in the room snapped out of their shock and congratulated her.

"Hey, why weren't we invited to the party?" Cassidy strolled in with a wide-eyed Beth by her side.

"Oh, my sweet girl." Judith stood with Kyle's help and joined Beth by the door. "How are you doing?"

Tears welled in Beth's eyes. "I'm fine. Cassidy has been a huge help."

In the short time he'd known Beth, she had a tendency to brush off attention to herself. Injuries included. Doug studied her for a moment to confirm her statement. The scrapes and bruises didn't signal any major concerns. And the doctors had tended to her arm where the bullet had carved a groove. No blood spotted the bright white bandage.

"That's good. Make sure my boys—" she patted Cassidy on the arm "—and my girl, take care of you." After a quick hug, Judith says her goodbyes.

"What did we miss?" Cassidy helped Beth to the chair beside Doug's bed.

"Oh, not much. Judith and Harold are engaged. That's all." Kyle shrugged, straining to keep a straight face.

"What!" Cassidy spun and stared at her fiancé.

The group exploded into conversation. Doug tried to follow the exchange, but his mind drifted with fatigue. Beth laced her fingers with his. He rolled his head to the side and peered into the most gorgeous green eyes he'd ever seen. A smile tugged on his lips.

She dipped her chin and batted her lashes. The insecurity in her gaze smacked him in the chest, stealing the air from his lungs. After witnessing her strength when they'd run from the shooter and her determination to get them down the river, he'd forgotten about her lack of self-confidence.

"Did you find it?" Dennis's voice pierced the invisible bubble around Doug and Beth.

He shifted his attention to his boss. "What did you say?"

A knowing glimmer flashed in Dennis's eyes. "I asked if you found the evidence."

"Yes. At least, we think so." He visually searched the room. "Where are my clothes?"

"Right here." Kyle opened a tiny closet and retrieved a bag containing Doug's belongings.

"Right front pants pocket."

Kyle withdrew his clothes. He slipped his hand into the indicated pocket and found the flash drive. He stuffed the pants back into the bag and handed the memory device to Doug.

"Thanks." He took the object. "We haven't had an opportunity to look yet, but I know it's not mine. I can only conclude Michael put it there for safekeeping."

Jason pinned him with a glare. "Speaking of, we will have a conversation about the cabin and your secrets. But we'll let you recover first."

Doug let his gaze bounce from one person to

the next before it landed on his partner. The hurt in Kyle's eyes gutted him. Above everyone else, his partner deserved an explanation. He nodded. "It's long overdue."

Beth's grip tightened in quiet support.

Dennis cleared his throat, bringing the awkward silence to an end. "Let's confirm the flash drive is the evidence against Wade that Tabitha risked her life for, then we can proceed from there." The sheriff held out his hand, and Doug placed the small device in his palm.

"Speaking of Michael, how is he?" Beth asked.

Jason folded his arms across his chest. "He's awake for longer periods of time but groggy. We've talked a bit. It doesn't take long for him to wear out. There are still gaps in his memory, but the docs are hopeful it's only temporary."

The relief flowing from Beth was palpable. "Can I see him?"

Jason's gaze flicked to Doug.

Far be it from him to say no. Beth had had enough people in her life who'd controlled her actions. He dipped his chin, giving Jason the go-ahead.

"I can arrange that." Jason rubbed the back of his neck. "I have Deputy Fielding guarding Agent Lane. It's late. I need to get home to say hi to my wife and baby girl and get some much-needed shuteye. When I return in the morning, I'll take you to visit him. Hopefully, by then, he'll have gained more strength."

Dennis clapped his hands and rubbed his palms together. "Here's the plan. Doug, you rest so you can get back on your feet. But hear this: you will let the rest of us do the heavy lifting in this case. You'll continue to watch out for Tabitha. I called the VSPD and requested Officer Davis to monitor your room until you leave. He's outside now. Jason has Agent Lane's back with the help of Deputy Fielding. Kyle, continue to keep tabs on Tommy Wade and his lieutenant, Clark Bretton. Plus, pull in whoever you need to tail those two lowlifes. Check with Deputy Lewis. I think he's free to help. I'll work on the flash drive. I'd like to allow Keith time with the twins, but if we need extra manpower, I'll give him a call."

A round of "yes sirs" filled the room.

Cassidy placed her fists on her hips. "What about me?"

"I want you to do what you do best."

Cassidy arched a brow.

Dennis chuckled. "Dig deep into Wade. I want a list of associates, along with every charge ever brought against him and why the district attorney can't get a conviction."

"One deep dive coming up." Cassidy pushed off the wall where she'd stationed herself after she'd arrived.

"All right, folks, my partner requires his beauty sleep." Kyle shooed everyone from the room. After a round of goodbyes and giving his fiancée a quick kiss, he turned to face Doug. "I'll get the nurses to adjust the chair into a bed so Tabitha can stay by your side."

Doug's shoulders sagged in relief. He wanted her to stay but had no idea how to broach the subject. "I appreciate that. I don't want her out of my sight."

"Figured. I'll see you tomorrow." Kyle squeezed Doug's lower leg and strode toward the door.

"Hey, Kyle."

His partner peered over his shoulder. "Yeah?"

"Thanks, man." He tried to convey his gratitude for helping him and Beth and his regret for not sharing his past in a simple look.

Kyle jutted his chin in acknowledgment and left.

"You have great friends." Beth's soft voice re-centered his focus.

"They're an amazing group." He clasped her hand. "You can trust each and every one of them."

She shrugged. "It's not that easy."

"I realize that." He'd proven that by keeping part of his past to himself. "The horrors you've lived through aren't easy to overcome."

"No, they're not. But between you and Michael, I'm starting to see that not everyone in life is out to use me for their own agendas."

He lifted their entwined fingers and kissed the back of her hand. "Beth, I'm falling for you, and I'll admit it scares me to death. I've dated since Christine's death, but no one has made me feel the way you do. Those pesky butterflies flutter in my belly whenever you're around."

She chuckled. A cute blush filled her cheeks. "I can relate."

"Good. Now that we agree on that, let's get the nurse in here to make your bed so we can get some sleep. If I know the team, they'll be anxious to meet and review the evidence in the morning whether I'm released from the hospital or not." He pushed the button for the nurse.

Beth's gaze traveled to the door. "Do you think we'll be safe?"

He hated to see her fear. "Honey, Officer Davis is a good man and an exceptional law enforcement officer. He'll protect us with his life if necessary." Doug believed that to the very fiber of his being.

"I don't want anyone to die because of me." Beth's breath hitched.

"Wade would be stupid to come after you here. Everyone will be fine." But if it meant Beth living free from the likes of Wade, he'd give his life to make it happen.

EIGHT

Saturday, 2:00 p.m.

Thankful the doctors released Doug to recuperate at home, Beth dropped onto his couch, leaned back, and stared at the ceiling. She grabbed a throw pillow and hugged it to her chest. The air conditioner hummed, filling the otherwise silent room. Her conversation with Michael Lane rolled on a loop in her head. His insistence that she trust Doug with all the evidence she'd procured nagged at her. But giving up her last hope of convicting Tommy scared her to death.

When she'd collected the videos of Tommy ordering his enforcers to kill and a couple of times that he'd personally murdered those who disappointed him, she'd found a way to copy the accounting books of his drug business as a backup way of taking him down in case the murders didn't stick. Beth had glanced at the financial reports and discovered the names, orders, and purchase amounts of his associates. Several of the identities shocked her. A judge, a couple of police officers, and a small-town mayor were only a few of those in business with Tommy. The man had connections on top of connections.

Michael had prompted her to hide the evidence of the business side of Tommy's crimes in case the murder charges somehow didn't stick. In that scenario, they'd bring separate charges against the man and had another way to attempt to shut down his business. Now, Michael wanted her to give up her safety net. Could she truly trust the detectives to put Tommy behind bars? Michael said so, but she couldn't quite muster the same confidence. Tears blurred her vision.

"Doing okay?" Doug lowered onto the cushions and adjusted his sling.

She rolled her head to the side and met his gaze. "I'm tired. But good." Beth gestured to his arm. "How about you?"

He shrugged and winced. "I can still protect you if that's what you're wondering."

"Not at all." Funny, she hadn't questioned his abilities or his determination. Maybe she'd already crossed the line of trust, and her mind hadn't caught up with her heart yet. "Even with your injury, you are more than capable of keeping me safe."

"I'm glad you think so." Doug crossed his

ankle over his knee. "Do you feel better after talking with Michael?"

Had she detected a touch of jealousy in Doug's tone? She shook off the absurd thought. "I do. He was adamant that I can confide in you—about everything."

Doug studied her a moment. "And do you? Have you?"

She sucked in an audible breath. How did he know how scared she was? *No. I haven't told you everything. I'm scared you'll push me away.* And that was the bottom line, wasn't it? She cared deeply for this man, and he'd rip her heart out if he rejected her. "Let's just say I'm cautious. Surely you can understand why."

"Of course. But please—"

The door clicked, and Doug's friends piled in the house. So much for peace and quiet. Beth sagged with relief that the group had interrupted Doug's request.

With chairs arranged around the room, the detectives, along with the sheriff, settled in.

Kyle strode in from the kitchen, his arms loaded with cans of Pepsi, root beer, and water bottles. "Found Doug's stash of drinks." He dumped them on the coffee table, grabbed a Pepsi for himself, and took a seat.

The front door opened again, and a man she'd never met strode in.

"Howdy, everyone."

"Keith, my man, how's it going? You're looking a bit tired there, partner." Jason gave the man a hug that ended with two slaps on the guy's back.

"Tired is an understatement." The man Jason called Keith grabbed a chair and sat.

"How are Amy and the twins?" Dennis asked.

"Doing well." Keith claimed a water bottle. His gaze met hers. "We haven't been officially introduced. I'm Keith. Jason's partner, and a friend of these lugs." He motioned around the circle.

"Nice to meet you. I'm Tabitha. But everyone knows me as Beth."

Keith nodded. "I've heard the backstory. Don't worry, these people are the best."

The unspoken promise that the detectives would keep her safe was loud and clear.

Doug scratched the stubble on his jaw. "Not that I'm upset, but why are you here instead of at home with your girls?"

Keith tipped his bottle toward Doug's arm. "Heard some maniac winged you and wanted to come lend my assistance. Besides, my dad was dying to play grandpa for a few hours."

"Ian sure loves his grandbabies." Cassidy smiled.

"That he does. When he hinted at more, I thought Amy was going to strangle him." Keith shook his head. "Not a smart thing to say to a woman who endured thirty-two hours of labor only to find out she had to keep going because of the surprise of baby number two."

Jason cringed. "Oh, please tell me he didn't do that."

"Yup, right there in our living room after we'd been up all night with the twins."

Jason threw his head back and howled. "The man has a death wish."

The group joined in the laughter.

Keith leaned forward and rested his elbows on his knees. "Enough about my family. Jason's given me the basics. I'm here to help. What's going on?"

Tabitha's heart swelled at the love these friends had for each other. What would it be like to be a part of a group like this one?

"Let's get to it then." Dennis popped the top on a root beer and took a sip. "I examined the information on the flash drive last night. It's pretty incriminating. As soon as we're done here, I'll get a warrant in the works for Wade's home and office. Although, his business will be tricky with the evidence we have."

"I'll feel better once Wade is arrested and convicted." Doug reached over and clasped Beth's hand. "Assuming we can find a judge and jury not associated with the drug king."

Jason closed one eye and squinted into the hole

of his can of Pepsi. His mouth twisted to one side as his gaze returned to the group. "I can't believe he has that many puppets in the region."

"Believe it," Tabitha whispered. Should she listen to Michael and tell them about the accounting evidence? She chewed on her thumbnail. A bad habit that Tommy made sure she understood how much he didn't like. She grimaced at the memory of how he'd *corrected* her behavior.

The conversation—centered on how to take Tommy down and what the detectives had to do to make it happen—faded into the background as Tabitha mulled over Michael's words of trusting Doug and his friends. Could she? Her stomach twisted into knots.

Doug retracted her thumb from her teeth. "Stop it," he whispered.

She flinched and hunched in on herself.

"Hey, I'm not going to hurt you." Doug's voice was low enough that no one else heard his words. He clasped her fingers and rubbed soothing circles on the back of her hand.

The comfort eased her battered nerves. But she hadn't missed Kyle's raised eyebrow at her reaction. She lowered her eyes to her lap, refusing to acknowledge the detective's unspoken question. The group sitting around Doug's living room had protected her and helped her without prying into her past. She had no reason to fear them. But old habits were hard to break.

"I sure wish we had the evidence to shut down Wade's drug business." Dennis rested his elbows on his knees. "I can't stand the thought of my daughters growing up with that slime peddling his wares of death. Even if he goes to prison for murder, his business will continue to run."

"I second that." Keith closed his eyes. "My son and daughters are little, but it still scares me."

The group grew quiet. Most stared at the floor, but all refused to make eye contact with each other. No doubt, having the same thoughts.

The fathers' pained words pierced Tabitha's heart with an invisible dagger. What about her child? It was time to trust these people. *God, I hope I'm doing the right thing.*

"I might have a way." Her soft voice seemed to echo in the quiet room.

Keith straightened in his chair. "What's that?"

Her gaze connected with each person and then landed on Doug. The moment of truth. Did she follow Michael's urging to trust these men and Cassidy? She sucked in a deep breath. "I have another hidden flash drive. It has a copy of Tommy's accounting spreadsheets for his drug operation that includes details of what and who."

Doug's eyes widened. "Why didn't you say so before?"

She yanked her hand away and hugged her waist, cowering from his outburst. Tears pricked her eyes.

"Beth, I'm not mad. Just confused. I'd like to understand why." His caring tone made her tears fall. "Oh, honey." He wrapped his good arm around her shoulder, pulled her to him, and held her while she cried.

When her sobs subsided, Dennis cleared his throat. "I'd like to hear the story behind the other set of evidence, if you don't mind."

She knew the sheriff wouldn't let her walk away without revealing the information, but she appreciated the kindness. She extracted herself from Doug and accepted a tissue from Jason. After drying her face, she exhaled. "As you know, Michael approached me about getting evidence of Tommy's criminal activities. At first, it terrified me to go against Tommy. I'd seen first-hand what the man was capable of and experienced some of it." She shivered at the memories. "But the time had come that I was willing to risk everything to get away from him, so I agreed."

"That's when you secretly videoed Wade?" Jason asked.

"Yes. He saw me as a ditz. A possession without brains. Using that to my advantage, I gathered enough proof of him ordering hits, and torturing and killing his employees who dared to disobey and sent them to Michael."

"Is that when he hid you?" Kyle had a casual look as he leaned back in his chair, but the intensity in his gaze said anything but that.

"Not quite. We met under the illusion of doctor appointments. That's when I told him I'd copied Tommy's financial records."

"Did Agent Lane ask you to get those?" Dennis asked.

She shook her head. "An opportunity presented itself, and I took it. Besides, I was dead anyway if Tommy found out about the videos." Only after Tommy had taught her a lesson with his fists, but she refrained from mentioning that part. "Michael worried about a leak in his department. He asked me to hide the accounting data and not mention it to anyone until he was sure that the video evidence would stand up in court and he had a solid case. At that point, he'd add the additional charges."

Doug held his slinged arm and shifted to face her. "We found the flash drive Michael hid. Where's the other one?"

"In a safe place." Tabitha had gone this far. Why not all the way. "I can take you to it."

"Do you know what's in the files?" Dennis rolled his can of root beer between his palms.

"His entire business. Well, the drug portion,

anyway. The information on it will help you know who to avoid. It has the names of judges, police officers, and mayors, along with other high-profile clients. You'll be able to take down the entire operation."

Dennis met her gaze. "I can't thank you enough for risking your life to put Wade behind bars."

Tabitha hadn't done it for herself. She'd lived her entire life with abuse and told that she deserved it, but the baby inside her didn't. She refused to allow Tommy to destroy the child physically and emotionally like he had her.

Cassidy, who had remained silent throughout the discussion, sat forward on the edge of her seat and clutched her hands between her knees. "I'm curious. Did something happen to cause you to risk everything?"

And there it was, the secret she'd avoided telling. If her past and her hesitations hadn't pushed Doug away, the reality of her situation would. He'd lived through the horror of losing his own son. He'd never stand by her, knowing another infant's life was in the balance.

What was that old saying? *In for a penny, in for a pound.* "Tommy had isolated me from friends. Not that I had any to start with, but I had co-workers. Then he…well, let's just say I didn't disobey him. However, he found reasons to ensure that I never would." This was it. She took a deep breath and placed a shaky hand over her belly. "I knew I had to get away the day I found out I was pregnant."

Doug's jaw dropped. "You're what?"

She cringed. "I couldn't let Tommy's evil touch my baby, so I made an agreement with Michael, and here I am."

The lack of response in the room stung, but Doug's silence shredded her heart. She leaped from the couch and paused. Manners had been beaten into her. "Please, excuse me." She dipped her head, rushed to the guest bedroom, and shut the door.

Shame and humiliation flooded her. The offended look on Doug's face would haunt her forever. She curled up on the bed and let the tears flow.

God, when will I ever learn? No man worth having will ever want me. Why did I let my heart get involved?

"Beth, wait!" Doug struggled to get up from the couch. His injury slowed him, and the woman he cared about had already shut herself in her room.

"Doug, don't. Let her have a moment." Cassidy's firm tone halted his actions.

Jason ran a hand over his face. "Did you see the need for permission and the submissive way she didn't make eye contact? Wow, Wade really did a number on her."

"Her entire life has been a lesson in pain." Doug wanted to kick himself for his reaction. The woman had enough self-doubt. But she'd shocked him with her pregnancy revelation, and his brain quit working. Yeah, he'd messed up big time.

"I take it you didn't know." Dennis broke through his thoughts.

Doug scooted back, but his gaze drifted to the hallway where Beth had disappeared before he focused on the group. "I had no idea. Although…" In hindsight, he recognized the signs. "Maybe I should have realized. But she never said a word."

Dennis leaned forward. "Is this going to be a problem?"

Would it? Doug wanted to say no, but fear clawed at his chest. "It's not going to be easy, that's for sure."

A throat cleared.

Doug glanced around the room at his friends' curious stares. He'd withheld pieces of himself from all of them except Dennis.

"What's boss man talking about?" Kyle's hurt tone stabbed Doug in the gut. The man was his partner. They had each other's backs. Shared worries and troubles with each other. Except for the cabin and this.

"You should have done this a long time ago.

It's time to tell them." Dennis's soft tone belied the command. His boss had held his secrets long enough.

He swiped a hand down his face. "As you all know, my wife was murdered while I was deployed."

The group nodded.

"The whole ugly story is that she witnessed Tommy Wade murder a man during a drug deal. Everyone else in the neighborhood refused to talk. But Christine, being Christine, refused to let Wade get away with murder. So, she agreed to testify. A day later, Wade or one of his enforcers broke into our house and murdered her."

"And you've felt guilty about it since you weren't there, and your specialty is security." Jason folded his arms over his chest. "We knew all that."

Wow, his easygoing friend had no intention of cutting him any slack. Doug exhaled. "What you don't know is that Christine was pregnant at the time."

Cassidy gasped. "Oh, Doug."

He gave her a sad smile. "I lost not only my wife but my unborn baby."

"I can't imagine." Keith's pained expression told Doug he understood.

Quiet descended in the room.

Dennis broke the silence. "Are you going to

be able to deal with Tabitha's pregnancy? The woman doesn't need misplaced hostility due to your unwarranted guilt."

Leave it to his boss not to pull any punches. Could he? The thought of failing another woman and child gutted him. But that was his problem. "It won't be easy to look beyond my inability to save my wife and son, but you're right about Beth. She deserves to be treated with kindness and not suffer from my attitude because of the past. I'll do everything I can to support her."

"Good to know." Dennis gestured toward the group. "Keep going. You owe them all of it."

"There's more?" Kyle's jaw clenched. Doug didn't blame his partner. The man had shared his entire life story with him when Cassidy resurfaced last Christmas.

"Agent Lane and I are Army buddies. We served together and stayed in touch over the years. Anyway, he approached me not long ago and asked if I wanted in on taking down Tommy Wade. Of course, I said yes. I wanted justice for Christine and my son. So much so that I didn't tell anyone." He met Dennis's gaze. "Not even our illustrious sheriff. Something I regret."

"Good," Dennis grumbled.

"I've worked on letting go of the guilt of failure. But as you all know and have experienced, giving it to God is harder than it should be." He adjusted the strap on his sling. "I can't fail another woman and unborn child again and survive the fallout. Now you know the background and why Beth's news of a baby is a concern."

"I guess I can understand that. We've all had heartbreaks in our lives." Kyle's features relaxed.

He and his partner needed to have a long overdue chat, but Kyle's attitude change relieved him.

"And what about the cabin?" Jason flicked a look at Dennis. "Did you know about that too?"

His boss nodded. "Not until recently, though."

"I can tell there's a bit of hurt flowing around the room, but to be honest, I'm too tired to go there." Keith ran a hand over his head, causing his hair to stand in funny angles. "However, I'd like to know what's up with the secrets."

"I never meant to keep things from you all." Doug shook his head. "No, that's not right either. I didn't want to revisit the pain, and telling my secrets would have thrown me back into the abyss that I'd finally climbed out of. I struggled for months with the loss of my wife and unborn baby. The guilt ate at me. I hadn't been there. I hadn't protected my family. When I could no longer deal with day-to-day life, I bought the remote cabin as a place to hide from the world. It became my sanctuary."

"I get it," Cassidy whispered. "A place to escape from life and breathe."

Kyle clasped her hand and nodded.

"We practically live on top of each other and are in each other's business all day, every day. A little separation once in a while is a good thing." Jason tipped back in his chair and folded his arms. "I'm sorry for getting on your case."

That right there was why Doug loved working with this group and was proud to call them friends. "I'm sorry for shutting everyone out. Can we agree to go from here?"

The group nodded.

"Sounds like a plan." Dennis, who had stayed quiet while the detectives cleared the air, sat up straight. "With that out of the way, let's get down to business. Keith, you're on the computer files once we obtain them from the search. You should be able to do that from your home office. Jason, you'll be with Kyle and me when we serve the warrant." Dennis glanced at his watch. "If I get it to the judge in the next couple of hours, I should have it tomorrow, so be prepared for my call. Cassidy, I know your job is cold cases, but—"

"I'm in. Tell me what you want me to do."

"You are on protection duty. I don't want anyone coming near this house."

"Done."

"Doug, clear the air with Tabitha, then get some rest. Tomorrow morning take her to retrieve the flash drive and bring it to the station.

Any questions?" Dennis made eye contact with each person.

The facts spun through Doug's mind. He pinched the bridge of his nose. The hinky feeling that something was off hit him again.

"Hey, partner, you have that look that something's not right." Kyle had always read him well. That's why they made a great team.

"We're so focused on taking down Wade that I wonder if we're missing a piece of the puzzle."

"Go on," Cassidy prodded.

"Think about it. We know Wade won't stop until Beth is back in his possession. And I do mean possession." Doug gritted his teeth. How anyone treated another human being like that was beyond his comprehension. "But the tactics seem odd. Think about it. A break-in, two attempted kidnappings, and the effort to kill her twice at the cabin and in the woods. Together they don't make sense. Why change methods?"

"Now that you mention it…" Jason cocked his head to the side and scowled. "What is Wade up to?"

"Not a clue, my friend. Unless he has inside information about the evidence, he's getting desperate and wants her dead, so she can't testify against him. But I can't figure out how he'd know about the videos. None of us would leak that. And the only other person is Michael, and he definitely wouldn't say anything." Doug's lungs chose that moment to quit functioning. He'd faced the same situation years ago. He prayed fervently for a different outcome. "Then again, maybe I'm paranoid. If he is escalating, the changes make sense."

"I'm not making assumptions. We work the evidence and research our suspects. As far as I'm concerned, anyone with a link to Tommy Wade is not above this investigation. I want Wade behind bars, but not at Tabitha's expense. We'll examine the accounting data after you retrieve it tomorrow." That was why Dennis made a great boss. He listened and narrowed down the facts.

"I appreciate the focus on Beth. And I understand why you requested I rest, but with the threat on her, I don't want to wait until morning to get the other flash drive." Doug hated the idea of prolonging taking Wade down.

"I'm saving my breath by not asking for an extra day. But you will take the evening off to recover." Dennis pinned him with a *don't argue with me*, boss look. "You need it. Tabitha needs it."

Doug couldn't deny the fatigue that hovered over him. And Beth, with her pregnancy, required rest. "Yes, sir."

Kyle clapped his hands and brushed them together. "All right, everyone. Clean up the living room so Doug doesn't add a coronary to his ailments due to the mess, then let's get to work and stop this maniac."

His friends made quick work of the cans and bottles and returned the chairs to the kitchen. One by one, they said goodbye, all except Cassidy.

She placed her hand on his good shoulder and jutted her chin toward the guest bedroom. "You need me to stay?"

"No, I've got it. I'm just trying to suck up my pride before I go apologize." Beth hadn't left the bedroom since her grand exit, and that worried him. "If things don't go well, I might need your assistance, though."

Cassidy smiled. "I'll go monitor the perimeter for a while. I have the key and code, so once you make nice with Tabitha, get some sleep." She motioned toward his arm. "I'm highly aware of how injuries can wear you out."

And she was. She sported the scars to prove it. "Think she'll forgive me?"

The detective gave him a sad smile. "I think Tabitha's confused and hurting. But she's not a stupid woman. Deep down, she knows the truth. It's her head that is struggling to come to grips with the fact that you have her best interests at heart."

He reached up and patted her hand that rested on his shoulder. "Thanks, Cassidy."

With a quick nod, she disappeared outside,

leaving him alone to face Beth. He pushed himself off the couch and made his way to the guest bedroom. He leaned his forehead on the door and closed his eyes. *I kinda messed up earlier. I could really use Your help to set things right.*

He inhaled and knocked on the door. "Beth, can we talk?" He waited a bit, but there was no answer. "Beth? Please let me in."

The knob jiggled and turned. The door opened. Beth's red, puffy eyes tore a massive hole in his heart. "I'm so sorry."

She lowered her gaze and shrugged.

"Honey," He placed a finger under her chin and lifted. "No matter what you believe, I'm here for you. You and your child. Don't ever think I'll turn my back on you."

"What about your unborn baby?" Her eyes searched his.

He now understood what it was like to be under a microscope. His words would dictate what happened next, so he chose his answer carefully. "I'll always regret what happened to Christine and my son, but that has nothing to do with you. I'm sorry I gave you reason to question my response. But know this. I will not let you face this alone." He held out his good arm, praying she'd allow him to comfort her.

Beth fell into his embrace. Her sobs shattered his heart. For Beth, he'd battle through any remaining doubts and fears to give her a life of freedom and joy. Tears soaked his shirt and warmed his skin. He rubbed small circles on her back. This woman had lived a lifetime alone, and he planned to put an end to that right now.

"I've got you." He kissed the top of her head and held her tight.

Doug vowed to never let this woman go, but the worry that Wade would slip through the cracks of justice and take Beth from him snuck in and sent a shiver down his spine.

How would he survive losing another woman he cared for if he failed?

NINE

The sheer exhaustion from yesterday lingered as Tabitha climbed into the SUV the sheriff's office had delivered to Doug's home. The sheriff had insisted they get a good night's sleep before retrieving the secondary flash drive, and she appreciated it. Yesterday had pushed her to her limits. She closed the door and leaned against the headrest. Her eyes burned from the tears she'd shed the night before. And her head pulsed with an ache from the crying jag. Doug had apologized and held her until she'd found enough courage to pull away. His warmth had seeped into the deep cracks of her brokenness. For the first time in—well, forever—she began to feel normal. But could Doug ever love someone like her? She sighed. Probably not—but yet...

Her mind twisted into a jumbled mess, playing the conversation, or lack thereof, over and over. Doug's silence after she'd told him about the baby still stung. However, she understood why he hesitated. The past hadn't been kind to either one of them.

The driver's side door closed, jolting her from her thoughts. He'd lost the sling today, saying he no longer needed it. She doubted it but had no desire to upset him by disagreeing. Doug cranked the engine. "Where to?"

"My rental house." Tabitha rolled her head to the side and stared out the passenger window. A dark cloud of soul-deep exhaustion hovered above, threatening to consume her.

Using the reflection in the windshield, she watched as he laid his arm across the back of the seat and twisted to see out the back window. He backed out of the driveway with ease. "Are you sure it's still there? Whoever trashed the place did a thorough job."

"I'm sure." She hadn't hidden the flash drive inside but outside in the backyard. Her gaze drifted to the passing scenery. Sidewalks and trees lined the streets. A few children played on the front lawns of the neighborhood. Their muffled laughter filtered in through the closed windows. What would a carefree youth have been like? She sighed. No use dwelling on the past. What's done was done. But that didn't stop the tears from pooling on her lashes.

"What are you thinking?" Doug flipped on the blinker and made a right turn.

She slipped a finger under her eyes, swiped away the tears, and then rolled her head to face him. "That all children should be free to grow up without fear. That's what I want for my baby."

"You'll be a great mom." Doug checked the mirrors and scanned the area.

An unladylike snort filled the SUV. "Right." Without a good role model, how would she know what to do?

"You will. You have two things you didn't have before."

She sat up straighter. "What's that?"

"Faith and friends." He flashed her a sooth-ing smile.

She considered his statement. True, she now had God showing her what unconditional love looked like. But friends? She wasn't sure about that one. "Are you still my friend?"

Doug's head whipped in her direction. "Why wouldn't I be?" He returned his gaze to the road.

Might as well speak the truth. Doug hadn't hurt her yet because of it. "I just thought you'd like to get rid of me after yesterday."

"Beth." He inhaled. His fingers drummed the steering wheel. "I might get upset at times, but that doesn't mean my feelings about you have changed."

"And what are those?" She held her breath, waiting for his answer.

He rubbed his hand down his jaw. "I'm still trying to figure that out. But I do know that I care about you—a lot."

She pondered his confession. He seemed like a good guy. Michael trusted him. And so far, he was nothing like Tommy. A tantalizing aroma wafted through the vents as they passed Main Street Eats. Funny. She missed her job as a waitress. What would it be like to stay in Valley Springs and get to know Doug better? "I care about you too. But I don't trust my judgment when it comes to—well, pretty much everything."

"You will. Someday." Doug parked in the driveway of her rental house and turned off the engine. They exited and met at the front of the SUV. "Lead the way."

Tabitha stepped to the backyard gate and halted. Her pulse ratcheted. The evidence was the last thing she had between her and her freedom from Tommy. What if someone had followed them? She frantically searched the area.

A hand warmed the small of her back. "It's okay. Cassidy made sure we didn't have a tail."

She whipped around to face him. "She was behind us?" How had she not known Cassidy had followed them? She shook her head. Some detective she'd make. With trembling fingers, she unlatched the gate and slipped into the backyard. The steady footfalls of the man who'd never left her side gave her courage. She skirted the patio and headed to a small birdbath tucked within a patch of irises. "It's under there." She gestured to the white pedestal with an attached bowl.

Before she knelt, Doug crouched and raised the edge of the birdbath. He retrieved the black device encased in a small plastic bag that held the remaining evidence. "Got it." He stood. "Anything else while we are here?"

"I don't have much. And the things I do have can wait. I want to get that—" she pointed at the flash drive "—to a safe place."

"Then let's head out." He cupped her elbow and escorted her from the yard. His eyes constantly scanned the tree line. She'd noticed his demeanor change once he had the evidence. The easygoing man had morphed into a ball of tension. She hated to admit it, but his seriousness about the situation gave her a measure of relief.

Once in the SUV and driving away from the house, she glanced at Doug. The muscles in his jaw twitched. He'd gone from calming her to strung tight within seconds of retrieving the flash drive. "What's wrong? You're as tense as a turkey at Thanksgiving."

Doug chuffed. His gaze met hers for a brief moment. "The guys are on their way to Wade's to serve the warrant. I plan to join them after I drop you off at Miss Judith's."

Tabitha's heart pounded. He couldn't be serious. He should still have his sling on and required several days' worth of rest. However, he'd never allow her to stop him from doing his job. But placing innocent people in Tommy's path? "No. It's bad enough you're injured and going after Tommy. But Judith and her friends…" She shook her head. "I don't want to put anyone else in danger."

Doug captured her hand and laced their fingers together. "Cassidy is on security, and trust me when I say the retirement community is a force to be reckoned with. I wouldn't take you if I thought for one minute others would get hurt. Please, trust me on this."

Her eyes focused on their linked hands. His gentle grip, odd to her. Tommy and the others in her life possessed her. Whether physically or emotionally. Doug's touch was caring, and he talked to her like she wasn't stupid. "If you believe it's safe."

"I do."

"All right. Do what you think is best." She nibbled on the thumbnail of her free hand. Astonished that he hadn't released his hold and worried about her agreement at the same time.

She stared at the passing scenery. Guilt niggled at her, and fear closed its tight grip around her throat. *God, please don't let this be a mistake. I don't want others hurt because of me. And please keep the men safe when they confront Tommy.*

Twenty minutes later, Tabitha said goodbye to Doug and sat on the couch catty-cornered to Miss Judith, head down, wondering why she'd agreed to be left with—in essence—a stranger. Then again, the entire Valley Springs Sheriff's Department were strangers. Or they had been.

"Beth, would you like anything to eat or drink?" Miss Judith's soft tone surprised her.

She snapped her gaze to the older woman. "No, thank you." She tilted her head and studied the town's grandmother. "You're different from what I've heard the guys describe."

The older lady cackled. "Oh, my dear child, you've hung around those boys of mine too long."

She lifted her gaze to meet Miss Judith's. "I don't understand."

"I think you do." The woman smiled. "We become what others expect of us, don't we?"

"I guess." Who was Beth kidding? She'd done that her whole life. And if her scars—inside and out—were any indication, she'd attempted and failed miserably.

"More than that, I give my boys what they need. Most of the time, it's a good swift kick in the rear." Miss Judith chuckled, then pointed her red-polished fingernail at Tabitha. "You, my darling, require something different."

"And what's that?" The older woman confused Tabitha.

Miss Judith stood and moved to sit beside her. She took Tabitha's hand in her frail one. "Love and a bit of tenderness. I get the feeling you haven't experienced much of that."

The woman had read her like a neon sign. Love had never been part of her life until Michael introduced her to God. "I…" Tears spill over Tabitha's lashes.

"Come here, honey." The older woman engulfed her in a hug.

Tabitha's horrible life poured out in her sobs.

Miss Judith held her tight. "Let it out, sweet thing."

Her head pounded, and her eyes stung, adding to the crying jag hangover from last night, but for the first time ever, Tabitha experienced the feeling of being cherished by someone other than God.

A handful of tissues appeared in front of her. Tabitha took them and mopped her face. "I'm sorry for getting you wet."

"I'd drown in your tears if it made your hurt disappear." The woman brushed her hand down Tabitha's hair. "Besides, crying isn't a sign of weakness. It's cathartic. God gave us tears. Why not use them to purge the ugly in life."

She gave the older woman a watery smile. "When did you get so smart?"

"They say wisdom comes with age. Well, I should be a genius by now." Miss Judith winked. "Now, tell me what's going on between you and my Doug. The entire time he's lived in Valley Springs, I've never seen him so out of sorts."

"I'm sorry." Tabitha bit her lower lip. She'd upset Miss Judith by hurting one of her *boys*. The concept of a special relationship with the woman disintegrated through her fingers.

"No, sweet girl. It's a good thing. Someone finally tilted that man's world on its ear. He's lived with his misplaced guilt for far too long." Judith patted her hand. "Now, I want details."

Relief flooded her system, and the glimmer of mischief in Miss Judith's eyes made Tabitha chuckle.

Miss Judith arched a manicured brow. "Stop procrastinating. Start from the beginning."

Tabitha settled into the corner of the couch. Her worries vanished like a morning fog. "Fine, but it isn't a pretty story."

"Life rarely is. It's how we respond to it that matters." Miss Judith shifted, giving Tabitha her full attention.

And wasn't that some serious truth. Tabitha

took a deep breath and told Miss Judith everything, from the horrors of her childhood to the revelation of her pregnancy. "So you see, I'm not sure Doug will want anything to do with me when this is over."

A huge smile graced the woman's face. "Sweetheart, that man is smitten whether he admits it or not."

Tabitha's pulse stuttered. She let Miss Judith's words fill the empty places in her heart. A relationship with Doug…could it happen? Assuming she made it out of Tommy's clutches alive, she'd risk heartache to explore the possibility.

"What are you doing here? I told you to stay with Tabitha and rest," Dennis growled.

Doug leaned against the SUV a block from Tommy Wade's estate, where his boss and co-workers waited to serve the warrant. "I have to be a part of the takedown, and you know it. I owe it to Christine. And don't worry. Cassidy has security while Beth has some one-on-one time with Miss Judith."

"I'm not worried about her. Cassidy can handle that." Dennis drilled him with a hard stare.

"Yeah, well, I'm fine." He'd lost the sling that morning. Sure, his arm ached, but the sleep had done wonders for his energy level. "Keith has the accounting flash drive and will deep dive into the financials to see if we have enough evidence to bring down the entire operation."

Dennis sighed. "At least you listened to some of my orders."

"I can't let Jason have all the fun disobeying you." Doug waggled his eyebrows.

"Who, me?" Jason grinned and placed a hand on Doug's shoulder, and squeezed. "Glad to have you, my man."

"So, what's the plan?" Doug itched to search Wade's home.

"Brentwood PD is letting us take point, but they are covering the rear of the house. Kyle's knocking. If someone opens the door, he delivers the warrant. If not, I give the orders, and we breach simultaneously with BPD. I don't trust the scum inside to play fair. Either way, we go in ready."

"Roger that," the three men said in unison.

They hurried to finish dressing out in tactical gear. Jason and Kyle chattered about nonsense, ribbing each other in a friendly fashion, their typical pre–search warrant ritual. Under normal circumstances, Doug would join in, but today his mind focused on the upcoming task. His body hadn't healed to the point he could ignore the aches and pains, but he'd never admit that to Dennis. Doug wanted to—had to—be in on taking down Wade. The man had taken Christine and his baby from him and had destroyed Beth, both mentally and physically, over the last few years. Christine deserved justice, and Beth deserved freedom from the nightmare named Tommy Wade.

Donning his Kevlar vest took longer due to his injuries, but Doug refused to allow his ailments to stop him. With the last strap secure, he opened the weapons case in his borrowed department vehicle. He racked the slide of his Glock and confirmed he had a bullet in the chamber, then slipped it into his holster and continued to secure the other weapons. All armaments in place, he patted the pockets confirming he hadn't forgotten anything.

Doug strolled to his partner's side. "Ready."

Kyle clasped the shoulder of Doug's uninjured arm. "Don't worry. We'll get him."

Jason placed a careful hand on Doug's other shoulder. "What he said."

The two stood like sentinels on either side of him, giving him the strength he hadn't realized he needed.

Sheriff Monroe joined them. "Jason, Doug, and I will spread out. Kyle, wait for my signal, then approach and serve the warrant." Dennis handed Kyle the document.

His partner tucked the official paperwork into his vest. "Copy that."

Doug placed his hand on Kyle's back. "Don't get dead."

"Now you tell me." His partner chuckled. Before Doug took his position, Kyle stopped him and met his gaze.

Unspoken words passed between them. Doug loved the man like a brother, and by the emotion in Kyle's eyes, he felt the same. Both were very aware of the risks today. "I know."

Kyle nodded. "Go, so we can take this slime down."

Doug crouched and hurried to his position. Once there, he gave his boss a thumbs-up and focused on the task at hand. Serve the warrant, and search the house, preferably without a shot fired. A hinky feeling made the hair on the back of his neck prickle.

God, please keep everyone safe.

Sweat trickled between his shoulder blades. The situation felt off. He fought the urge to move but trusted the men he worked with.

Kyle strode up the walkway with an air of attitude. The man's head slightly shifted from side to side, no doubt scanning for trouble. He reached the door and knocked. "Police! Open up! We have a search warrant!"

Seconds ticked by.

The wait made Doug's internal *danger* meter spike.

Kyle knocked again. "Poli—"

Wade's second-in-command, Clark, flung open

the door, gun in hand. His eyes snapped to Kyle. He whipped his weapon at the detective. Kyle dove off the porch.

Doug launched to his feet and pulled the trigger on his Glock.

Clark's weapon dropped, and the man crumpled to the ground. He howled in pain, clutching his chest. Blood from the gunshot wound spread across the man's shirt. Doug had gone against his training and aimed at the man's shoulder. He wanted the man alive. He wanted answers. But Clark had turned as Doug pulled the trigger, and his shot hit the man in the chest.

"Jason, you have Clark." Dennis continued toward the house—gun raised.

"On it, Sheriff." Jason stalked toward the injured man.

"Kyle, are you okay?" Dennis's focus never wavered from the front door.

"I'm good." Kyle dusted himself off, scowling at the road rash on his arm. "Let's get Wade and get this done."

Leaving Jason to secure Clark and call an ambulance, Doug joined Dennis and Kyle and prepared to enter the house.

Gun at the ready, Doug extended his arm, eased the door open, and stepped inside. The others followed. Each cleared a room as they continued down the hall. "Search warrant!" Kyle tapped his shoulder and motioned at a short hallway to the left. Doug nodded and continued straight ahead with Dennis at his back. Muffled voices rose from the back of the house. Doug blocked the Brentwood officers out of his mind. They'd take care of others on the property. His focus stayed on his task. Securing Tommy so they could safely search the house. "Wade!"

Tommy Wade stepped from the kitchen. A handgun aimed at Doug. "Don't come any closer, Detective."

"Stand down. We have a search warrant." Doug stared at the man, refusing to flinch. The game of chicken came to mind, and he didn't intend to lose.

A sneer crossed the drug king's lip. "Don't believe anything that tramp told you. She's worthless. Only good for one thing."

Anger coursed through Doug's veins, knowing what the man had done to Beth. "This isn't about Tabitha. This is about you paying for your crimes."

A sly smile bloomed on Wade's face. "Ah, yes. How is your wife doing? Oh, that's right. She's dead. My condolences."

Doug's grip tightened on his Glock. He waged war on his desire to pull the trigger.

"Doug." Dennis's warning kept him grounded. He valued life more than the lowlife in front of him. He wouldn't stoop to the creep's level. "I'm good, boss." Out of the corner of his eye, he spotted Kyle slip behind Tommy. He had to keep Wade occupied so the man didn't notice his partner. "I have you to thank for that, don't I?"

"Why, Detective, I have no idea what you're talking about." The drug dealer laughed.

God, this man is not making it easy for me. Please, give me self-control.

Doug forced himself to continue engaging with the monster in front of him. Kyle only needed a few more seconds. "I'm sure you don't. You probably had someone else do your dirty work for you. It's not like you have the courage to do it yourself." Okay, so taunting the man probably wasn't the best idea.

"You think I won't kill you right here and now?" Wade's voice rose, and his finger tightened on the trigger.

He stared Tommy down, his own finger on the trigger of his weapon.

Kyle slipped in from the side. One hand gripped the top of the gun near the barrel, the other at the back near Wade's hand. In one quick motion, his partner yanked down and back, jerking the weapon away.

Tommy spun. His right hook connected with Kyle's jaw, sending his partner sprawling across the floor.

Dennis rushed in, took the drug dealer to the ground, and cuffed him.

"You okay, Kyle?" Doug holstered his Glock. His hands shook. It wasn't the first time he'd had a gun pointed at him, but the look of pure evil in Wade's eyes had sent his pulse racing.

"Yeah, I'm good." His partner patted his jaw. A red mark, sure to leave a nasty bruise, began to swell. "You?"

"Same." Doug slapped Kyle's back.

Dennis kept his gun leveled on Wade in case the man decided to be stupid. "Brentwood cleared the rest of the house and have several workers in custody."

"Come on. Let's go see what BPD scooped up." Doug's adrenaline faded, and he fought the exhaustion taking over.

Dennis lifted Wade to his feet and gripped the guy's elbow. The sheriff quoted the Miranda rights as he escorted the drug king outside while Doug and Kyle followed, watching for trouble.

Once Dennis stuffed Tommy into the back of a patrol car, he strolled over to join the Brentwood PD officers. "How many?"

Sergeant Titus folded his arms across his chest. "We found four while you all were dealing with Tommy."

"Anyone you think might be involved?" Dennis asked.

"In general, no. We'll question the chef, maid, and gardener, but in my opinion, they're only guilty by association." Titus rocked back and forth on his heels. "Now the accountant, on the other hand, is acting a bit squirrely."

"Sheriff."

Dennis held up a hand, staying Doug's comment. "Sergeant, I'd appreciate it if you'd let us sit in on the interview with the accountant. We have reason to believe he's hiding something."

Titus narrowed his eyes. "Anything I should know about?"

"Not at this time. My people are still digging into the possibility."

The officer grunted. "A seat at the table is granted. But keep me informed so I'm not blindsided by anything."

"Of course. And thank you, Sergeant." Dennis shook the man's hand. When the officer strode away, the sheriff gestured toward Kyle. "Get some ice on that. And Doug, since you shot Clark, I'll need your weapon."

"Yes, sir." He secured his weapon and handed it to the sheriff. "I know I'm on administrative leave until the investigation is complete, but I'd like to be included at the conference table when you review Wade's interrogation."

"I'm not concerned about the investigation. It's a formality. You saved your partner's life.

You'll be cleared." Dennis's brow furrowed. He appeared deep in thought. "I'll allow you to be a part of the conversation—after the interrogation. I'd like Tabitha there too. She might shed some light on things."

"Thank you." The review of his actions hadn't worried Doug, but to hear his boss agree lifted a huge weight from his shoulders.

Jason strolled over and eyed Kyle's jaw. "Looks like you're losing your edge there, buddy."

Kyle opened his mouth, but Dennis held up a hand and stopped the teasing before Kyle responded to the taunt. "What's the update on Clark?"

"Not looking good." Jason glanced over his shoulder at the ambulance pulling away from the scene. "I handed over babysitting duties to one of Brentwood's finest."

Dennis nodded. "I'll check on the man's condition later. Until then, Jason, you're with me. We'll ensure the warrant is handled and a thorough search is underway, then we'll meet Doug and Kyle at the station."

"Sounds like a plan." Jason clapped Doug on the back. "Wade will not get out of this one."

"From your lips to God's ears." Doug had hit his limit on excitement. His limbs had turned mush. "Kyle, mind driving my vehicle?"

"Can do." His partner waved at Dennis and Jason. "See ya at the station."

The officers and deputies that filled the yard parted as the two men ambled to the SUV. Blue and red lights bounced off the trees and surrounding buildings. Energy sapped, Doug climbed into the passenger side and rested his head against the back of the seat.

The SUV driver's door closed and the engine started. "You don't look too hot there, partner." Kyle shifted into Drive and pulled away from the scene.

"I've been better. The past couple of days are catching up with me." That and wondering if he'd ever see Beth again. Nothing like having a gun pointed at you and seeing your life flash before your eyes to make you consider your future.

"Well, things are looking up. Clark and Wade are both in custody, along with the accountant." Kyle tapped the steering wheel with his thumbs.

"True. But we have to make the charges stick."

"We will, buddy."

"I hope so. Beth's freedom hinges on it." He shifted his gaze out the passenger window and watched the landscape flow by.

The events of the past couple of days, plus the evidence gathered, ran on a loop in his head. It all seemed straightforward, but what if they'd missed something?

TEN

Sunday, 4:00 p.m.

Doug left his empty holster in the SUV before he and Kyle took over the Brentwood PD conference room. He felt bare without his duty weapon, but rules were rules. The coffee bar on the counter that lined one wall had called to him, and he'd made good use of it. An infusion of caffeine was what the doctor ordered. Well, maybe not, but it should have been. He dropped into a padded swivel chair similar to the ones at ACSD. The cushiness eased his aching muscles. A slight breeze from the air conditioner gave the room a touch of chill. He wrapped his hands around his cup and absorbed the warmth.

Ice pack to his face, Kyle leaned back in his chair and closed his eyes.

"How's the jaw?" Doug lifted the mug to his lips and sipped the dark brew. *Not bad for PD coffee.*

His partner opened his eyes and peered at him. "The man caught me off guard."

"I didn't say anything about how you got the bruise, just asked how it felt." Doug smirked.

"Sore, but I'm sure you can relate."

He grunted. Oh, without a doubt, he could. "Think Brentwood's finest will get anything out of Wade?"

"I certainly hope so." Kyle lowered the ice. "Tabitha's on her way?"

Doug nodded. "I talked with Cassidy when we got to the station." He glanced at his watch. "They should be here any minute."

The two detectives let a comfortable silence settle between them. The events of the day had taken a toll.

Kyle exhaled. "Do you love her?"

Doug snapped forward in his chair, instantly regretting it. He blew out a long breath, tamping down the discomfort. "Where did that come from?"

"I've seen the way you look at her. How you defend her." Ice pack on his jaw, Kyle's gaze met his. "Don't let your guilt get in the way of a good thing. Take it from someone who's been there."

"What are you now, my therapist?" He settled back into his chair but couldn't deny Kyle's words. The man had allowed anger and guilt to consume him. He'd almost lost his fiancée Cassidy in the process.

"Nah, man. But I like seeing you happy. And she makes you happy."

He couldn't deny that Beth made his heart beat a little faster. That her sweet demeanor drew him in. And the protectiveness that boiled inside when he recalled the abuse she'd endured was off the charts. "I'm not sure it's love, but yeah, I like her a lot."

The door eased open. Cassidy and Beth stepped inside.

One look at Kyle and Cassidy strode to his side. "Did Doug finally get tired of your ridiculous self?" Her words belied the worry in her eyes.

"Wade might have gotten in a surprise punch before we took him down." Kyle smiled at his fiancée and winced.

Cassidy shook her head. "I'd say." Her fingertips traced the darkening bruise. "Are you really okay?"

Kyle grasped her fingers and kissed the back of her hand. "I'm good. I promise."

The worry Cassidy had sported on arrival bled out.

Beth stood at the entrance of the room, hugging her waist. "Is he really in custody?"

Doug pushed from his chair and stepped in front of her. He ran his hands up and down her arms, trying to chase away the fear glimmering in her eyes. "He's in interrogation as we speak.

Dennis is listening and will bring us the information." He guided Beth to the table. "Have a seat. It shouldn't be too long before we hear something."

He retrieved a water bottle for Beth and sat next to her while Cassidy poured herself a cup of java. "So, how'd it go with Miss Judith?"

The smile that graced Beth's face made his heart soar. "She's a wonderful lady. Not at all how you all portrayed her."

Doug tilted his head. "What do you mean? That woman doesn't pull punches with anyone. We love her to death, but man, can her words sting."

"Only because they're true." Cassidy lifted her coffee in a salute.

"You have a point." Doug chuckled. He adored Miss Judith and would do anything for the woman, but he couldn't deny her words of wisdom and truth tended to lay a person's heart bare for a thorough examination.

A smile blossomed on Beth's face. "I'm not sure what all you are talking about. She was so sweet with me."

The group stared at her. They all loved Miss Judith, but the word *sweet* had never crossed their minds.

"Seriously, she was amazing and so delightful."

"This I've got to hear." Kyle waved his hand in a rolling motion, urging her to continue.

Beth obliged and amused them with her time spent with the older woman.

Conversation ceased when Dennis strode into the room. He closed the door, tossed his notepad on the table, and collapsed onto a chair.

"Hey, boss man. How'd it go?" Kyle rested his ankle on his knee.

"PD is still talking with Wade, but so far, they haven't gotten much out of him. His attorney Danielle Thompson is a piece of work. She definitely knows his business and is preventing him from answering questions that will incriminate him."

Beth snorted. When all eyes turned to her, she ducked her head. "Sorry."

"You obviously have an opinion. What is it?" Dennis's tone softened.

"Let's just say she's very aware of what happens in that house."

Doug shifted to face her. "What do you mean?"

"I might have been his possession, but she's his mistress, and Spencer Hayes, the accountant's, mistress as well."

"Death wish much?" Kyle shook his head and mouthed, *wow*.

Doug had a hard time processing how anyone would willingly risk punishment and cross Wade like that. "Does Wade know about the accountant and his attorney?"

Beth shook her head. "No. Because if he did, the accountant would be dead."

"Not the attorney?" Cassidy asked.

"No. She's too important. She keeps him out of jail. He can't afford to lose her."

Dennis stroked his chin with his thumb and finger. "I want a deep dive into Ms. Thompson and the accountant."

"I'll take that assignment. As soon as we're finished here, I'll request a computer and workspace." Cassidy made a note on her cell phone.

Doug's phone buzzed. He glanced at the caller ID and answered it. "Hey, Keith."

"I found something interesting in the accounting files."

"Hold on. Let me put you on speaker." Doug tapped the button and set his phone on the table. "You're on with Dennis, Kyle, Cassidy, and Beth."

"Like I said, I found something in Wade's financials."

"Go on." Dennis rested his forearms on the table.

"I don't know who, but someone is siphoning money from Wade's accounts. It's little amounts at a time, and since it's going into the miscellaneous column, it probably isn't alerting anyone.

It's disappearing between the ledger and the bank statement. Unless someone is looking for it, they might miss it with the high dollar amounts of Wade's business we are talking about."

"The accountant?" Kyle asked.

"Spencer Hayes? Possibly. I don't see how he'd miss the discrepancy. Being how that's his job and all." A baby's cry filled the line from Keith's end. "Hold on… Okay, I'm back. Sorry, that was little Miss Stacey making her presence known."

"No problem. Let me text Jason with the information. He's with the team questioning the accountant right now." Doug grabbed his phone and shot off the message.

Dennis stood and paced the length of the room. "Tabitha, you lived in that house. What do you think?"

Beth's eyebrows rose. "Me?"

The sheriff nodded.

She chewed on her lower lip.

Doug laced his fingers with hers. "Beth, honey. It's okay." The timidness in her gaze tore him to pieces, but he knew his tiger was in there somewhere.

Her gaze locked on their entwined hands. "I can't see Spencer stealing. He's a bit of a weasel but no backbone."

"And the affair with Danielle?"

"I didn't say he was smart. But if I had to

guess, that's her doing, and he's going along with it for obvious reasons." Beth shrugged. "You have to admit, the woman is beautiful."

Kyle grunted. "Looks are not a good reason to risk your life."

Jason entered and made a beeline straight for the coffeepot. "Wade's accountant, Mr. Hayes, was a wealth of information."

"How so?" Dennis returned to his seat.

Coffee in hand, Jason joined the group at the table. "He confessed about redirecting the money. However, he swears it's not for him but won't say who's benefiting from the cash. Unfortunately, BPD doesn't have enough evidence to hold him, so they're releasing him in the next half hour or so."

"Do you think he's responsible for Beth's attempted kidnappings?" Doug hated for the man to go free until they figured out who had targeted Beth.

Jason took a sip. "Not sure. But it goes back to why. Kill? Sure. Eliminate a witness? I can buy that. But kidnap? I don't think so. What's the purpose of that?" The harsh inhale of air had the man jerking his head toward Beth. He cringed. "Sorry, Tabitha."

She tucked her chin down and peered up at Jason through her lashes. "No need to apologize."

Doug glared at Jason. At least the man had the

decency to look remorseful. "We should look into everyone associated with Wade." Doug placed his hand over Beth's. "Please write down all the players in his organization, including his chef and housekeepers. I don't want to skip over anyone."

"I can do that. But I don't know who he does business with." Beth accepted a notepad and pen from Cassidy.

"Don't worry about those, Tabitha. I have that information from the flash drive you supplied," Keith said. "While Tabitha takes care of that, I'm going to drop the call and continue to examine the financials. Talk to y'all soon."

When the call disconnected, Doug pocketed his cell phone.

As if on cue, Dennis's phone rang. "Sheriff Monroe." The man's shoulders sagged. "Thank you for letting me know." After hanging up, Dennis steepled his fingers and tapped his chin. "That was the officer on guard duty at Brentwood Community Hospital. Clark didn't make it."

Beth's head jerked up. Tears swam in her eyes. Without a word, she returned to writing the list. At least she was free from the man.

A jackhammer took up residence in Doug's head. He'd taken a life. Granted, he'd saved his partner's, and Clark was scum, but still. He massaged his forehead.

"Doug, you did what you had to do. I wouldn't

be alive right now if you hadn't taken that shot." Kyle's tone soothed the edges of Doug's battered heart.

"Thanks, man." The room grew quiet, except for the scratch of the pen Beth used to write names. He appreciated the silence to center his mind. A few moments later, he turned his attention to the woman beside him. Her shoulders slumped, and a mask of exhaustion covered her face. "If it's okay with you guys, I plan to take Beth home to rest once she finishes the list."

"I agree." Dennis pointed at Doug. "You *both* need to take a break. We'll call if we find anything important. Otherwise, I'll see the two of you at the office tomorrow morning. We should have more detailed information about Wade's businesses by then."

Beth placed the pen on the notepad and slid it to Cassidy. "That's everyone I can think of."

Cassidy scanned the names on the paper. "Great. I'll get on this list and make profiles of those we don't have yet."

"I guess we'll see everyone tomorrow." Doug pushed from his chair, his muscles protesting. He bit back a groan and held out a hand to Beth. "Shall we?"

She nodded and exited the room with him. They walked to the parking lot, both lost in thought.

Once in his SUV, she shifted to face him. "Do you really think I'm safe now that Tommy is behind bars and Clark is gone?"

"I honestly don't know." Doug's heart plummeted at the thought of losing her. His pulse quickened. What if he lost Beth and her baby the same way he'd lost Christine and their son? He refused to allow that to happen. "But I can promise you this. I'm not leaving your side until we know for sure."

Tabitha swallowed hard. Had Doug realized what he'd committed to? Her gaze drifted from the front windshield to the side mirror and back. Tommy was behind bars, and Clark died of his injuries. The two men she feared the most were no longer a threat—at least for the moment.

"I'm sorry I dragged you into my mess." The guilt had piled on with each threat that had come her way. Doug didn't deserve to suffer because of her poor choices in life.

He reached across the console and laced his fingers with hers. "You didn't pull me in. I came after you, remember?"

"How could I forget? You pushed your way into my life and haven't given up." That moment in the parking lot after she'd seen Clark had given her hope. Michael had disappeared, and Doug had come to her rescue. "At the time, I believed you only wanted my help to get justice for your wife."

He lifted her hand and kissed the back of it. "While it's true that I do want that. Christine did the right thing and unfortunately, paid the ultimate price. But you, Beth, deserve to live a life of freedom surrounded by those who care about you. Please don't ever forget that we have your back—I have your back. You are no longer alone."

His words, a balm to her aching heart. She squeezed his hand. "Thank you."

He flashed her a smile.

The cars on the highway ahead slowed and came to a stop. Doug pressed on the brakes. "Looks like there's an accident about ten cars up." The crease in his forehead deepened.

"What's wrong?" Beth strained to see what had worried Doug.

"I'm required to assist, but I don't want to leave you alone."

"Go. You need to help those people. I'll be fine. Wade's in custody. I'll lock the doors and stay in the car. I promise." His genuine concern for her tugged at her heart. He really did care.

"I don't have much of a choice. Keep your cell phone handy. I'll be back as soon as possible." He glanced at her. The war between staying and going evident. He finally huffed and got out. He stuck his head through the opening. "Lock up." And with that, he closed the door and strode toward the accident.

Beth pushed the button, and the locks clicked. Alone for the first time since Doug came into her life, she rubbed her small baby bump. Most wouldn't notice, but she had. Her maternal instincts had kicked in the moment she'd found out about the little life inside her. "Hang on, little one. It's almost over. Then we'll be free."

The truth knocked the air from her lungs. Once they had Tommy in prison and his drug business dismantled, Doug and the others would leave her life too. The thought disappointed her. She'd come to enjoy the tight-knit group. Especially the handsome detective that had stolen her heart. What if she told him that she wanted more? Was it too soon for him? And what about her horrible life choices? Could she trust herself?

"Argh!" She lowered her head into her hands and gripped her hair.

The driver's side window exploded, and a bullet pierced the passenger window.

Tabitha's body shook. Someone had shot at her. If she hadn't leaned down... Her stomach roiled and threatened to empty. She hadn't heard anything except the glass shattering. A suppressor? Why else wouldn't she have heard the blast from the gun?

Tabitha peered up from her bent-over position. A figure stalked toward the car. The sun shadowed the person, making it impossible to identify the shooter. She'd promised Doug she wouldn't leave the SUV, but staying wasn't an option. Surely, he'd understand and wouldn't punish her for disobeying. She gritted her teeth at the ridiculous thought.

She flipped the locks, flung open her door, and tumbled to the ground. Heart pounding, she scrambled toward the woods that lined the highway, keeping the vehicle between her and the shooter for as long as possible.

A ten-foot gap stood between her and safety. She inhaled. *God, I need Your help.* She sprinted across the open area. Her foot slipped, and she stumbled. She threw out her hand to catch herself, then half ran, half crawled the final distance. The hard thud of boots behind her pushed her faster.

A bullet pinged on a tree trunk near her head. Her cheek stung from the wood slivers that flew in multiple directions. A quick swipe of her face streaked blood across her hand. Great. More wounds to add to the mix.

She ducked her head and continued deeper into the woods, zigzagging through the trees. Praying Doug heard the windows breaking, she hopped over fallen limbs and slapped at branches reaching out to grab her. Her heart pounded, and she struggled to pull air into her lungs. Doug would save her like he'd done over the past few days. She just had to believe—had to stay alive until he came to her rescue. Five, maybe ten minutes later—she'd lost track of time—she tucked behind a thick bush. Her breathing came in short pants.

Twigs and branches meshed into a tangled wall hiding her from whoever chased her. She slid to the ground, tucking into a tight ball, and closed her eyes. The person who'd shot at her had a familiarity, same as the person from the cabin, but her mind refused to put the pieces together. Too small for Wade or one of his goons. A bit delicate, but muscular. Spencer. Brentwood PD had released him around the same time she and Doug left the station. But that didn't make sense unless he was responsible for stealing the money and thought Tabitha knew about it.

"Doug, where are you?" she whispered. Tears filled her eyes. Wade was in jail, and her freedom remained out of reach. She bit back the sob that threatened to escape.

Footsteps crunched on the leaf-lined ground, moving closer to her hiding place. "Tabitha, you can't run forever. You might as well give up now."

That voice. She knew that voice. But it couldn't be right. Why come after her?

* * *

The glorious sound of fire truck sirens signaled their approach. All Doug wanted was to get back to Beth, but he couldn't leave. Not yet. He lay on his stomach with his legs sticking out from beneath an overturned minivan and patted the little boy whose screams had threatened to shatter Doug's eardrums. "The firefighters are almost here. They'll get you out. Hang tight, little man. I'm going to tell them to come get you."

"Promise?" Tears and snot covered the young boy's face.

Doug grabbed a blanket that stuck out from the child's car seat and wiped the kid's nose. "Promise. Can you be brave while I tell them where you are?"

The child's lower lip stuck out in a pout, but his head bobbed up and down.

"Good. Everything will be okay." Convinced the boy wouldn't lose it again, Doug wiggled out from under the vehicle. The gravel on the shoulder of the road dug into his elbows and knees. Thankfully, the boy trapped in his car seat was scared but didn't appear seriously injured. Doug stood and dusted off his pants.

"Sir!" A man jogged toward him.

"Can I help you?" The tension carved on the guy's face sent a shiver of apprehension up Doug's spine.

"Is that your sheriff's vehicle?" The man pointed to where Doug had left Beth in his SUV.

"Yes. Why?"

"Someone shot at it, and a woman ran into the woods." The man pointed to the thick of trees near his SUV.

Doug grabbed the man and gave him a gentle shove toward the wrecked car. "There's a boy in there. Make sure the fire department knows." Doug sprinted toward where he'd left Beth and skidded to a stop. Shattered glass littered the ground, and the passenger door stood wide open. "Beth!"

His hand flew to his holster and came up empty. He yanked his cell phone from his pocket and punched the speed dial for his partner.

"Howard."

"Kyle, Beth is gone." He spun in a slow circle, searching for any sign of her.

"What do you mean gone?"

"Someone shot out the windows in the SUV. Her door is open. She's not here!"

"Hold up. Start from the beginning."

Doug blew out a long breath. Waiting went against everything in his being, but he had to be smart. "We were on our way to my house, and there was this accident on the highway. I had to leave her to help…first responder and all that. And now she's gone."

"Yeah, I got it. Go on."

"A man came running over and told me someone shot at my SUV. When I got back to the vehicle, Beth wasn't there." He ran shaky fingers through his hair. "Kyle, I need backup."

"On it. Just a sec." Kyle must have lifted the phone away from his mouth. "Hey, guys, Beth's in trouble…yeah, on the highway…got it. Doug?"

"Yeah, man, I'm here."

"We're on the way. Ten minutes out."

To make it ten minutes, they'd have to go lights and sirens. "Thanks." He hung up. He had to pull himself together before his friends joined him. Steady and chill. That's what they all tagged him as. So much for calm. His heart raced, sweat beaded on his forehead—and not from the August heat. While Doug waited for his friends, he examined the scene, talked to witnesses, and worried about Beth until his stomach twisted into a knot worthy of a Boy Scout.

Red and blue lights flashed in the distance, accompanied by the ear-piercing whine of sirens. He swallowed the fear creeping up his throat.

Doors slammed, and his friends raced toward him.

"Run it down again." Dennis's no-nonsense tone grounded Doug.

He paced a six-foot path while he repeated the series of events.

Kyle's phone rang. "Hey, honey… Cassidy, we're a bit… Okay. Guys, Cassidy has news." His partner put the phone on speaker and held it in his palm. "Go ahead, Cassie."

"I started my deep dive into Wade's employees with the accountant Spencer Hayes and the attorney Danielle Thompson. I'm glad I did."

"Is Hayes behind this?" Doug asked.

"Quit interrupting."

"Sorry."

"Anyway, Hayes is being threatened."

"By Wade for an affair with Danielle?" Kyle asked.

"No. By Danielle. Either he does what she asks, or she'll tell Wade that Hayes is embezzling his money."

"So, it's the accountant behind the attacks on Beth?" Doug clenched his fists.

"No. Quite the opposite. Hayes is only guilty of cheating on his wife out of fear, not attacking Beth."

Doug wanted to scream at Cassidy to spit it out. They didn't have time for dramatics. "Then who's doing it and why?"

The voices and chaos in the background faded, and he hyper-focused on Cassidy's voice. "I'm still digging, but from what I can piece together, Wade's attorney is the one responsible for terrorizing Beth."

Kyle's gaze connected with everyone in the circle around his phone. "Cass, I know you're good at your job, but give us a little more to go on than that. What are we up against?"

"And quick. Beth is out there, and who knows what's happening to her as we stand around here chitchatting." Doug's patience wore thin. The detective in him knew they needed the information, considering the level of the previous attacks, but the man in him was desperate to find the woman he cared about.

"Keep your shirt on," Cassidy huffed. "Here's the thing. I've conferred with Keith, and from what I've uncovered, Danielle is stealing from Wade. She's using the accountant to maintain her secret. And with the two of them sharing a bed, she has Hayes's life in her hands. If Wade found out, he'd blame Hayes for seducing Danielle, not the other way around."

Doug shook his head. "I'm not sold on that. Whoever tried to kill Beth had skills. Not everyone can handle weapons and make explosives. Plus, the person who came after us through the forest knew how to track. The attorney doesn't strike me as having those skills."

"Are you saying women can't do those things?" Cassidy practically growled the words.

"Not at all, but Danielle seems too prim and proper for all that." Doug had made Cassidy mad, but at the moment he didn't care. He wanted answers.

The detective mumbled something about men. "That's where things get interesting. Danielle, aka Danny Thompson, is a panther in a kitten's body. Raised by her militia father, that woman has more weapons training and bomb-making skills than most law enforcement have in their big toe. That's why I called. Be careful. Danielle is deadly, and I don't want to see any of you hurt while rescuing Beth."

Dennis rubbed the back of his neck. "Understood. Thanks, Cassidy. Keep digging. I want everything you have on Danielle Thompson."

"Will do, boss. I'm out." Cassidy hung up.

Kyle stuffed the phone into his pocket and turned his attention to Doug. "Now that we know what we're up against, let's get out there and find the woman you love."

"I don't—" Doug froze. He could deny all he wanted, but the truth hung in the air. "You're right. I love her, and I'm terrified I'm going to lose her."

"We'll find her." Dennis patted his back. "Do you have your personal backup weapon?"

"It's in the glove box."

"Get it. And I want vests on. If it *is* Ms. Thompson, and she's as trained as Cassidy says, I'm not risking anyone's life."

"Yes, sir," the men said in unison and followed orders.

Doug hurried to the SUV and retrieved his Sig Sauer. He donned his vest, then clipped the conceal carry holster to his waistband. He joined the team at the edge of the road. "What's the plan?"

"If she's as good as Cassidy claims, everyone be careful. Sheriff, why don't you and I go left." Jason drew his Glock, held it next to his leg, and gestured to the woods. "While Kyle and Doug remain partners and go right." Jason and Dennis took off.

"Kyle, it's been over twenty-five minutes since Danielle shot at her. I shouldn't have waited to go after her."

"And if you had, you might be dead. Then what good would you be to her? You did the right thing by waiting for backup." Kyle backhanded Doug's arm. "Come on, partner, get your head in the game, and let's go get Beth."

Doug strode next to his partner toward the woods. Kyle was right. He had to pull it together. He inhaled and blew air through pursed lips. Falling apart wouldn't help Beth. And from what Cassidy had told them, he had to utilize every bit of his training to defeat Danielle.

ELEVEN

Sunday, 8:30 p.m.

The sun had all but disappeared—a blessing and a curse. Tabitha rested her back against an oak tree and tilted her head, listening for her attacker. Emotion clogged her throat. The more time that passed, the closer she came to giving up hope. Exhaustion had taken over, and her determination to win the battle dwindled. Tears pricked her eyes. How had her life become one disaster after another?

She pinched the bridge of her nose, staving off the waterworks threatening to fall. She never would've guessed Danielle Thompson for a killer. But then, being pregnant and hiding in the woods hadn't made her list either. What had she done to put her in the attorney's crosshairs?

Tabitha slipped from her spot and continued to move. Staying in one place had certain death written all over it. One thing she'd learned, Danielle's prim and proper exterior was a façade. The woman hunted like a pro, and Tabitha's role of prey made her skin crawl.

"I know you're out there." Danielle's voice whispered through the darkening evening, taunting her.

Losing the battle of holding her tears at bay, they streamed, unchecked, down her cheeks. Danielle had played with her since the moment she ran. Tabitha had no way out, and time was not her friend. She survived her childhood and escaped Tommy's clutches with Michael's help. Doug had protected and assisted in Tommy's arrest. And when she thought her life had turned a corner for good, she'd die just out of reach of the man she'd come to love.

Doug, where are you?

Footfalls sounded to her right. Tabitha took off as fast as possible in the dimly lit woods. A sprained ankle or broken leg, highly probable if she stepped wrong. Panting from exertion and fear, she ducked behind a boulder. *God, I'm alone and scared. I could really use Your presence right now. Help Doug find me, and please protect my baby.*

Something scraped a few feet away. Tabitha whimpered at the unfairness.

A hand shot out and grabbed her by the throat. "Gotcha." Danielle's eyes had a bone-chilling dullness. "Thought you'd escape from me, didn't you?" The woman's long, manicured fingernails dug into Tabitha's skin.

She clawed at the woman's fingers closing off her airway. Dots peppered the edge of Tabitha's vision.

"Police! Let her go!" Doug's baritone voice echoed through the trees.

Danielle shifted and wrapped her arm around Tabitha's neck. The barrel of a handgun pressed against her temple. "I suggest you put your weapon down, Detective." The woman's calm demeanor terrified Tabitha.

Doug held his gun steady. "You know that's not going to happen."

"Then she dies." The sneer in Danielle's voice sent icy fingers dancing up Tabitha's spine. It was only a matter of time before the woman lost all touches of reality.

The barrel of the gun dug deeper into her temple. Tabitha whimpered.

Fire lit behind Doug's eyes. "It will not end well for you if you don't put down your weapon."

Danielle laughed. "Nice try, Detective."

"I know about the affair with Spencer Hayes and the money. You aren't getting out of this." Doug moved slowly to the right. "But there's something I don't understand. Why try to kill Tabitha?"

An unladylike snort came from the attorney. "She knew my secrets. I could manipulate the outcome with her under Tommy's control. But when she left, I couldn't risk it."

"I didn't know anything." Tabitha struggled to force out the words.

"Liar!" Danielle pressed the gun harder into Tabitha's skin.

The woman had hit the point of becoming unhinged. Tabitha realized that her time on earth was up. She had so many regrets in life, but there was one she refused to leave unsaid. Unafraid of Doug's response anymore, she wanted to take the leap and put her heart on the line. Tell him that she loved him. The arm wrapped around her throat made it impossible to voice the words, but she'd do the next best thing. Her gaze met his. She mouthed, *I love you.*

His eyes widened. A hardened resolve replaced the concern. "Give it up, Danielle. You're surrounded."

Three men decked out in Kevlar vests and black tactical pants emerged from the depths of the trees. All aiming handguns at Danielle. Help had arrived. The only problem…the woman held Tabitha close, making it impossible for any of them to take a shot without hitting her.

"No!" The woman's feral cry made the remaining air whoosh from Tabitha's lungs. Danielle's chest rose and fell against her back at a rapid pace.

The sheriff edged closer. "You have no way out. Let Tabitha go and put your weapon on the ground."

Tabitha gasped as the woman's intent flashed through her. The woman had a way out—killing both of them.

The woman shuffled and faced Kyle as he spoke. "Do the smart thing and surrender." Danielle's body relaxed, but she never released the tight grip on Tabitha.

Doug moved into Tabitha's line of sight and mouthed, *When I say to, drop.*

Her heart rate kicked up a notch. Could she do what he asked? Doug had called her a tiger. Did she have that strength inside? The thought of her baby slammed into her. She had to do it— had to be strong. Determined, she blinked twice, acknowledging his command.

He gave her a quick nod letting her know he understood.

"Release Tabitha so we can all walk out of here alive," Jason piped in.

Hands gripping Danielle's arm, Tabitha watched a wordless conversation between the men. Jason kept the attorney's focus on him while Kyle holstered his weapon.

Her pulse rate skyrocketed. Whatever the guys

had planned was about to happen. She clenched her muscles and glanced at Doug.

"I will not let her go! She will die!" Danielle's body vibrated with hate.

Doug met Tabitha's gaze. "Now!"

Tabitha relaxed her muscles to dead weight and prayed.

The moment Beth dropped, the world spun in slow motion. Doug and Kyle sprinted for the duo. They had to reach the women before Danielle regrouped. His command for Beth to drop to the ground, the hardest one he'd ever given. He prayed he hadn't gotten her killed.

Kyle flew from one side, tackling the attorney, and Doug from the other, grabbing Beth and taking her with him. He hit the ground first to protect her and the baby, rolled, and covered her with his body. He tucked her head under his arm and turned to witness a battle that would make a professional fighter proud.

Danielle flung her fist, aiming for Kyle's head, and kicked at his partner with a determination born from desperation. The woman was a scrappy thing as the pair struggled to claim the weapon. Grunts and heavy breathing filled the air.

He had to help his partner. "Beth, stay down!" He lifted to his knees.

The gun went off.

Muffled shouts from Dennis and Jason swarmed in his ear like a handful of wasps. Doug sat with a thud and slid sideways to the ground. He inhaled, but air refused to enter his lungs. Gasping, he fought to breathe.

"Doug?" Beth's voice floated in the air. "Are you hurt?"

Yes. No. Yeah, he had no idea. All he knew was that he couldn't breathe.

"Dennis!" Beth's frantic tone made his heart ache.

He wanted to answer her, but for the life of him, his mouth refused to cooperate. Darkness closed in on the edge of his vision. His body rolled. A searing pain lanced through his torso. Had the bullet ripped apart his chest?

Hands patted him. "No blood. Doug, can you hear me?"

He gave his boss a quick nod. Or at least he thought he had. Man, it hurt to breathe.

Dennis squeezed his shoulder. "The bullet hit your vest. No holes, but it'll hurt like crazy."

No kidding. A hot poker had nothing on the searing pain.

Dennis unstrapped Doug's vest and pulled it off. "There. That should help."

The relief was immediate once his boss removed the weight of the vest. A few shallow breaths cleared his vision. Then he took a couple of deeper ones. Finally, he exhaled. "Help me up." Dennis stood on one side, Jason on the other, and they eased him to a seated position.

"Good?" Jason crouched next to him.

"I think so." The pain had eased a bit, but he wouldn't soon forget the equivalent of getting hit in the chest with a sledgehammer.

Beth cupped his cheeks and gently pulled his attention to her. "Don't scare me like that."

"I didn't intend to worry you." His gaze drifted to her mouth, and he wondered how soft her lips would be on his. He was a cad for thinking about kissing her in the middle of the woods after Danielle threatened to kill her. But he could have lost her, and he was tired of second-guessing himself. "But I *do* intend to kiss you." He waited for her to decide if she wanted what he offered.

Instead of drawing back, she leaned in and pressed her lips to his.

He wrapped his arms around her, ignoring the burn of his newly acquired bruise, and deepened the kiss. When he pulled away, he rested his forehead against hers and struggled to catch his breath. This time for a whole different reason. "That, sweetheart, was pure bliss."

A smile graced her face. "I completely agree."

Jason grunted. "I never thought I'd see the day."

"What do you mean?" Kyle asked. "My partner isn't a monk. He's dated before."

"Well, you do have a point. But seriously. Did you see that kiss?" Jason whistled between his teeth. "Wowzer."

Doug hadn't taken his eyes off Beth and tried to block out the conversation going on around him.

Sheriff Monroe approached and folded his arms. "If you two yahoos are done with your comedy act, I want the both of you to transport Danielle back to the station. Take Jason's vehicle and leave the other for Doug."

"On it, boss." Jason's tone turned serious.

Ignoring the razzing, Doug stole a quick kiss. The idea of having Beth in his life had his smile growing. He pushed to a stand and groaned. Hand pressed against his chest for support, he helped Beth to her feet and tucked her in beside him. Pain aside, he aimed to show her how a gentleman treated a lady.

Kyle patted his back, then joined Jason in escorting the attorney toward the road.

"Sheriff, I'd like to take Beth to the hospital and get her checked out."

"I agree. Head to Valley Springs General. And while you're at it, have them take a look at you too." Dennis held up his hand to stave off Doug's argument. "You've been beat up a lot lately, and that bullet to the Kevlar vest will leave a mark. A simple checkup won't hurt. I'll meet up with you later."

"Fine. But Beth and the baby come first." He refused to risk her life or her child's.

"Of course." The sheriff glanced around the scene. "I'll call in Deputy Fielding to cover here and collect evidence. I don't want Ms. Thompson getting off on a technicality."

Doug placed his hand on Dennis's shoulder. "Thanks for everything."

"That's what this team does. We help each other." His boss clasped Doug's fingers. "Now go and take care of your lady."

He swallowed the emotions clogging his throat. "Come on, Beth. Let's get out of here."

She wrapped her arm around his waist and met his stride.

As they marched through the woods, he steered her around downed limbs to avoid twisting an ankle, but her quietness worried him. A few minutes later, his concern peaked. "Beth, honey, what's wrong?"

"I—" She sniffed. "I was so scared."

He tightened his hold, offering her his strength. His chest screamed at him, so he focused on the pathway to shove the deep ache away while letting her process without interruption.

"I prayed you'd find us. And even though I

feared for my baby's life…" She rested a palm on her belly. "It killed me inside that I hadn't released my fears and insecurities and told you how I felt."

His steps faltered. The jolt had him hissing against the discomfort. "And how do you feel?"

She pivoted and locked her eyes with his. "Doug, I've never loved or been loved by anyone my entire life, starting with my mother. Michael introduced me to God, where I discovered an unconditional love that I still don't comprehend at times. But it changed my life. It wasn't until you that I trusted enough to allow my heart to explore the true meaning of love with another person." She gripped his fingers and brought them to her chest. "I love you, Doug. I know you might not feel the same, and that's okay. But I can't go another minute without saying it out loud."

Tears stung his eyes. He'd feared failing another person he loved, but gazing into the depths of Beth's green eyes drove out all doubts. "Beth, words can't describe the power of your trust in me. I've struggled for years with guilt that if I ever loved again, I'd fail. But you've shown me I can be the man God made me to be without fear." He brought her hands to his lips and kissed her knuckles. "I love you too, Beth."

Her contented sigh made him smile.

"What do you say we get you to the hospital

and make sure you and baby are fine? After we're both checked out, then we can go home, rest, and discuss what's next in our life."

"Sounds wonderful. I'm tired, hungry, and ready to put this all behind me." She tugged at him to continue the trek back to the road. "Do you really think I'm safe from Tommy and Danielle?"

"I think ACSD won't stop until we know for certain." Doug refused to allow another person in Beth's life to take advantage of her. The idea of her spreading her wings and learning to fly under his love and that of his friends filled his heart to overflowing.

And if Tommy or Danielle beat the charges, he'd work night and day to protect Beth from the monsters who'd tried to destroy her.

TWELVE

Two weeks later

A haze swirled in Tabitha's head. Doug had stood beside her during her sonogram and held her hand. The same hand that now warmed the small of her back as they meandered down the hospital hallway to Michael Lane's room. She itched to pull the picture of her baby from her purse and stare at it. According to the doctor, her baby girl was healthy. And if her daughter's somersaults were any indication, she was quite happy in her current home.

Doug whispered into her ear. "Thank you."

Her forward motion stopped. She blinked, struggling to connect the dots. "For what?"

He shifted to face her and cupped her cheek with his palm. "For letting me come with you to your appointment."

Without thinking, she leaned into his touch. "I hope it wasn't too hard for you."

A silent moment lingered between them. He

cleared his throat. "I can't say that my heart didn't hurt for my son, but when your little girl filled the screen, and you smiled… I realized God gave me a gift. Two, in fact. You and your baby. And I intend to enjoy it and not let the past dictate my happiness."

Staring into his brown eyes, she saw a myriad of emotions. She'd suffered from a cruelty that no one should experience, but his life had held an agony of a different kind. "It's okay to grieve—to remember. I won't hold that against you."

Relief flashed through his gaze and vanished. "And I'm sure I will. Especially now that Wade is behind bars and I have closure in my wife and baby's death. But I refuse to let it control me. You deserve more." He kissed the top of her head. "Come on. Michael's up and around. Doc says he'll discharge him tomorrow." Doug laced his fingers with hers, and they continued down the hall.

Michael Lane had changed her life. She owed him everything. Including the relationship she had with Doug. If Michael hadn't told her to trust him…nope, she refused to go there. No more second-guessing herself. Well, not as often, anyway.

Standing outside the hospital room door, Doug slid his hand up her back to her shoulder. "Are you ready?"

She nodded. "Knock-knock." Tabitha poked

her head inside Michael's hospital room. "May we come in?"

"Tabitha. Doug. Yes, please." Michael scooted to an upright position. The bruising on his face had faded to a lovely yellow green. "It's good to see you both."

She hurried to his side and gave him a hug. When she pulled back, their gazes locked. "I can't thank you enough for saving my life in more ways than one."

The man blinked, opened his mouth, and closed it.

Tabitha laughed. "I never thought I'd witness that."

Michael scrunched his forehead. "What?"

"You at a loss for words."

The agent rolled his eyes. "Very funny."

Doug joined her at Michael's bedside and shook the man's hand. "Looking better, my friend."

"Feeling better too." Michael clapped his other hand on top of their linked ones. "I appreciate you stepping in and helping Tabitha."

Doug wrapped his arm around her waist and pulled her in close. "Trust me, it wasn't a hardship."

"Oh, I see how it is." Michael chuckled. "Do I get credit for playing matchmaker?"

"Whatever makes you feel better," Doug teased.

Michael turned serious. "Sheriff Monroe came by and updated me. I'm happy to hear that Tommy Wade is behind bars, but I'm sorry I was out of it and couldn't warn you about his attorney Danielle Thompson. I figured out that piece right before someone tried to blow me up."

"I'm glad they didn't succeed." Doug caressed her arm as he spoke to Michael. "By the way, your little tip to Beth about a leak at your office helped plug that hole. Your boss never would have investigated your department without it."

"Yeah? Did they figure out who was tipping off Wade?"

Doug nodded. "Avery."

"The new guy?"

"Apparently, one of the bigwigs planted him on your task force for the very reason of keeping Wade out of jail. Now that we have threads to pull, the entire organization is unraveling as we speak."

Michael's attention shifted to her. "What about you, Tabitha? Is everything okay?"

"Everything's fine. We're all alive, and that's what counts." Tabitha refused to let either man wallow in guilt. "To answer the question that you are tiptoeing around, the baby is good."

Michael's shoulders relaxed. "I'm glad."

"Me too." She swiped at the tears pooling on her lashes. Stupid hormones.

Doug tugged her and pressed his lips to her hair. When his cell phone buzzed, he released her and pulled it from his pocket. "Olsen…sure, give me a minute." He returned his attention to her. "I have to take this, but I won't be far."

"Go, do what you have to do. Michael and I have some catching up." She patted his arm.

He feathered a kiss on her cheek and strode out of the room.

"So, what's going on between you and my Army buddy?" Michael's cheesy grin made her laugh.

"I know it sounds ridiculous, but I love him. And he says he loves me." She continued to worry that her happiness would vanish, but she'd chosen to trust God with her future.

"I have never known that man to say something that isn't true. In fact, during our time together overseas, he tended to be brutally honest."

A smile bloomed on her lips. "He went with me to my sonogram appointment today."

"He did, huh? How's the baby doing?" Tabitha hadn't missed the smirk on his face.

"*She's* fine." Doubt found a crack in Tabitha's new self-confidence and wiggled in. She shifted her gaze to the floor. "Michael, am I making another mistake?"

"With Doug?"

She nodded.

"Tabitha, look at me."

She lifted her gaze.

"Don't second-guess what you and Doug have. Sometimes it takes people months or years to figure it out, and sometimes they just know. If I had any doubts about that man, I'd speak up. But there's one thing that I'm certain of."

She nibbled on her thumbnail. "What's that?"

"Your heart is safe with him."

"You really think so?" Tabitha knew the answer, but she needed the confirmation.

"I know so."

She closed her eyes. "Thank you." Hearing it from Michael eased any lingering reservations.

"Anytime." Michael rested back against his pillow. "Now that we have that settled, tell me what's happened since they arrested Wade."

Tabitha scooted the chair next to his bed and lowered onto the cushion. "Once the chaos died down and the sheriff's department deemed it safe, I moved back into my rental. I have another month on the lease you paid for to figure things out. I still have my job at the diner, so I'll have an income. Not much, but some. After that, I'm not sure." She shrugged. "I want to stay in Valley Springs. The people here are amazing. But beyond that, I don't know."

"That's a start." Michael retrieved the cup and straw from the roller table over his bed and took a sip. "I'll help any way I can. If you need another month or two of rent, I'll take care of it."

She swallowed the emotion threatening to bubble out. "I don't know how to thank you."

"That's easy. Have a wonderful life with Doug." The grin on Michael's face made her laugh.

The door swung open. Doug's laidback demeanor had shifted to all business.

One look and her heart thundered. Her fingers dug into the arms of the chair. "What happened?"

His long strides ate up the distance, and he knelt beside her. He took her hand in his. "Wade is dead."

A whimper fell from her lips. Her nightmare was gone. Black spots danced on the edge of her vision.

"Breathe, honey." He tucked a wayward strand of hair behind her ear. She inhaled, pushing the darkness away.

"How?"

Doug's gaze connected with Michael's then shifted to her. "A gang member took him out. From what Brentwood PD has pieced together so far, Wade killed the guy's brother. It was retribution, plain and simple."

"He'll never hurt me again?" She clasped her shaking hands together in her lap.

Doug's thumb caressed her cheek. "Never."

She stared at him, waiting for the punchline to a bad joke. Was it really true? "And my baby will be free?"

"Beth, Tommy Wade is gone. You can live without fear of him."

She struggled to wrap her mind around his words.

"What about Danielle?" Michael asked.

"That's another story. But I don't see her escaping the charges against her. Besides, she was only a threat to Beth while Wade was alive."

Tears poured over Tabitha's lashes. She buried her face in Doug's chest and sobbed.

He wrapped his arms around her and held her shaking body. "Shh…you're safe now." He squeezed her tight. "I've got you, honey. And I don't plan to ever let go."

For the first time in her life, Tabitha experienced freedom. No more being used by others, just the feeling of love.

Doug handed Beth a glass of iced tea and joined her on the couch. After promising to stay in touch on a more regular basis with Michael, he and Beth had come to his house to rest. At least, that was his excuse. He wanted time with her, and to be honest, he needed a moment to process what he'd experienced at her sonogram appointment.

A baby girl. Between the little limbs and heartbeat, he'd struggled to not become a blubbering mess. He smiled at the memory. "Now that Wade is gone, what would you like to do?"

"Funny, Michael asked me the same question." She sipped the tea and placed it on the end table before shifting to face him. "I know I want to stay in Valley Springs. You see, there's a certain detective that I'm a bit fond of."

"You don't say." He grinned like a fool at the declaration.

"Yeah, he's kinda awesome." Her eyes dropped to her lap, and pink infused her cheeks.

He loved her bashfulness. She'd come such a long way in a short time. On occasion, she'd flinch, or the ingrained submissiveness would rear its ugly head, but her confidence had flourished. His butterfly had spread her wings, and any day now, he'd see her soar.

Beth tucked her leg under her. "Beyond that, I have no idea. I really do like working at the café. Maybe I'll keep that job. It doesn't pay much, but I've lived on a lot less before."

"If you could choose anything in the world, what would it be?" He clasped her hand in his. "Dream big."

She nibbled on her lower lip. Her forehead scrunched. "Anything?"

"Yup."

"You'll think it's stupid." And there was that subservient mindset again.

"Never."

"I know I'm supposed to want a career." Her fingers splayed on her belly. "But more than anything, I want to stay home and care for my baby."

"There's nothing wrong with that." Doug placed his hand over hers. "I think it's a great idea."

She shook her head. "I can't for multiple reasons." Her eyes glistened with unshed tears.

"Talk to me."

"For starters, I have to provide for us. Plus, I can never let anyone have that much control over my life again."

Doug thought about the future. One that included her. But he understood her fear and would never ask her to be that vulnerable again. It hurt knowing where the need came from, but he was man enough to swallow his pride and support her in whatever made her feel secure.

The air conditioner kicked on. The whoosh of air through the vents broke the silence. "What if you could have both?"

Her eyes snapped to his. "What do you mean?"

He took a deep breath. *Here goes nothing.* "We've lived through a lot over the past several weeks. I feel a connection with you I haven't felt since Christine. You're the piece of my life I've been missing, and I don't want to ignore what God has given me—you."

"Doug?" Her green eyes widened.

He stuffed his trembling fingers into his pocket and retrieved the small velvet pouch. If she said no, he'd ask again and again until she said yes. He'd visited Miss Judith a few days ago. She'd set him straight and erased all his worries about proposing. Then she'd shocked him by giving him her original wedding set. The woman told him, *I'd be honored if you gave her my ring. An heirloom of sorts. That girl deserves roots. Something she's never had before.*

He pulled the antique-looking princess-cut diamond from the protective pouch, slipped to the floor, and got down on one knee. "Beth, I realize how sudden this might be, but I know what I want, and I'm not going to wait because of others' opinions. I want to show you what real love is. I want to be the man you turn to in good and bad. I want to raise that baby girl of yours together and call her mine. And just maybe give her a brother or sister or two." He closed his eyes for a moment, gathering courage. "Miss Judith gave me her ring to give to you so you'd have the depth of a family. She wants you to have it, and so do I. Beth, will you marry me and make me whole again?"

Streams of tears streaked down her face. "Are

you sure? I come with a lot of baggage. I might not ever fully recover from my past."

"I've never been so certain in my life. And honey, we'll face the future together, no matter what it holds."

"Then, yes, I'd be honored to be your wife." Her arms flew around his neck, and she planted the most delicious kiss on his lips.

He slipped the ring on her shaky finger.

She lifted her left hand and smiled. "It's perfect. And so are you."

Doug's life had come full circle. He'd lost his wife and unborn son. And through the grace of God had a second chance with Beth and a baby girl he vowed to love and protect.

EPILOGUE

March 8, 3:00 p.m.

Tabitha gazed out Jason and Melanie's kitchen window and lifted her iced tea. The ice cubes clinked on the side of the glass as she took a sip. She smiled at the antics of Dennis and Charlotte's girls and the two dogs in the backyard. The group decided to celebrate Miss Judith's birthday in the only way those men and women knew how—a loud, joyous get-together. Tabitha leaned her hip on the counter and shifted her gaze to her husband and infant daughter in the living room. Doug tucked the pink blanket around Hope and swayed back and forth while chatting with Kyle. When Hope whimpered, he switched from swaying to bouncing. The man was a natural as a father.

Her thumb rubbed the wedding set on her left hand. The sensation a new one. Due to swelling during her pregnancy, she had to remove the engagement ring and wear it on a chain around her neck. Then when they'd married on New Year's Day, since the wedding band wouldn't fit on her swollen hands, she'd slid it onto the chain as well. Doug had married her and jumped with both feet into his role as husband. He'd been fantastic during Hope's birth. Once their daughter arrived, they both cried at the new life and for Doug's son, taken too soon.

"You look happy." Miss Judith poured herself a drink and joined her at the counter.

"I am." She tipped her glass toward Doug. "He's a great husband and father."

"All my boys are." Judith took a sip, grabbed a paper towel, and wiped the condensation from the glass. "Marriage and parenthood looks good on both of you."

Tabitha shifted to face the older woman. "As it does you. I think you surprised everyone by getting married over Thanksgiving."

Miss Judith chuckled. "Harold, the old coot, said he wasn't getting any younger and wanted to enjoy every minute we have left on this earth. Who was I to say no?" Did Tabitha see a hint of pink in the older woman's cheeks?

"Admit it. You wouldn't have it any other way." Miss Judith had a different kind of relationship with her than she had with the others. Tabitha saw a softer side of the woman. A sweet grandma she never had. The whole department considered Judith the spunky no-nonsense grandmother, but to Tabitha, she was the kindest, gentlest woman she'd ever known.

Miss Judith nudged her shoulder. "You are correct, my girl."

Her heart filled to overflowing at the endearment. She belonged to a wonderful patchwork family.

"What do you say we go see that granddaughter of mine?"

Tabitha raised a brow. "Which one?"

The pair laughed.

Judith shook her head. "This group is making up for lost time on the baby front."

"And you love every minute of it." She couldn't help but smile. Something she'd done a lot of lately.

"That I do." Judith offered her elbow to Tabitha. "Come on. Let's join the chaos."

She accepted the gesture and strode with Judith into the living room. An octagon fence-type playpen sat off to the side. Keith and Amy's eight-month-old twins, Stacey and Ellie, squealed with delight at the toys in the enclosure. One of the girls tossed a stuffed bear over the edge. Amy retrieved it and handed it back to the little darling.

Miss Judith veered toward a very pregnant Charlotte. Dennis's hand rubbed small circles on his wife's back. He kissed her cheek, whispered in her ear, then sauntered toward his detectives, who stood in a semicircle where they could keep an eye on everyone. The group was a protective bunch.

Little hands patted Tabitha's legs. "Up, pease." Noelle, Jason and Melanie's fourteen-month-old, held her arms up. Tabitha adored how the little one said please.

Grateful her doctor had released her for normal activity a few days ago, she obliged the toddler. "How's Miss Noelle today?"

The girl patted Tabitha's cheeks. "Cookie."

She laughed. "I think we need Mommy or Daddy's approval for that."

"Momma!" Noelle wriggled, wanting down. Tabitha held on to the girl until the little one had her balance before letting go. On a mission, the toddler ran to Melanie.

Tabitha glanced at those she now called family. Love and friendship as thick as molasses filled the room. Growing up, if someone had told her she'd understand the true meaning of love, she'd have walked away in disbelief. This—in front of her—was all she'd ever wanted.

Thank You, God, for giving me my heart's desire.

Blinking back tears of joy, she strolled to her husband's side.

* * *

Doug's new daughter, Hope, snuggled against his chest as he chatted with the others. The little girl sucked on her fist. The slurping sound made him smile. So much had happened over the last six months it had made his head spin—in a good way. Judith and Harold's wedding at Thanksgiving, and Kyle and Cassidy's at Christmas. He and Beth had decided to marry on New Year's Day so their baby girl would have his last name. However, the paperwork for him to officially adopt Hope was still in the works.

Beth's arm slid around his waist, and she leaned in and kissed Hope's silky head.

He smiled. Beth was an amazing wife and mother. She'd worried at first since she hadn't had good role models, but with the support of his friends and her natural instincts, she had thrived as an attentive wife and caring mother. He thanked God every day for the opportunity to see her blossom into the woman He'd made her to be.

Dennis strolled to the group and motioned to Hope. "She looks good on you."

He couldn't contain the smile that tugged on his lips. "I couldn't agree more. I'm hoping to talk Beth into a dozen more."

Beth groaned. "Can we please wait a while before we discuss having more?"

"I'm just teasing." He swooped in and kissed her breathless. "I'd like more, but I want to love on our little girl for a while first."

"Good." Beth rested her head on his upper arm.

"This group is becoming quite the baby factory." Keith gestured toward all the children around the room. "Who's next after Charlotte and Dennis have theirs?"

Jason caught Dennis's gaze. "Is Charlotte going to make it through the next few weeks?"

"I don't know." Dennis rubbed the back of his neck. "That son of ours is already worrying me. She started having mild contractions a couple of days ago. Doc told us he doesn't think that little boy will listen to reason and will make his appearance a bit early."

Kyle laughed. "First, Amelia the brainiac and now a strong-willed son. At least Kayley is normal."

"You'd think. But that girl is sneaky. She has manipulation down to an art form." Dennis dropped his head back and stared at the ceiling. "What did I ever do to deserve this crazy in my life?" The question held a satisfaction that even the sheriff couldn't deny.

"And you love every minute of it." Keith nudged his boss's shoulder.

"You bet I do." Dennis took a sip of his drink.

"So, who's next? Kyle, are you and Cassidy planning on having kids?"

"We are. But I'd like to enjoy at least a year of wedded bliss before we add to the chaos."

Jason cleared his throat, gathering everyone's attention. The room grew quiet except for the young ones playing. Melanie joined him at his side. He tugged her in close. "First of all, I'd like to wish Miss Judith a very happy birthday."

Everyone raised their cups, and a round of agreements filled the air.

"We've had a lot to celebrate lately, and Mel and I would like to add to the mix." Jason beamed at his wife. "We had a bit of a surprise a few months ago."

Melanie laughed. "That's one way to put it."

"Spit it out, dude," Kyle huffed.

A huge smile spread across Jason's face. "Mel and I are pregnant."

"Congrats."

"Congratulations."

"That's awesome."

A variety of well-wishes sounded from the group.

Keith arched a brow and smirked. "You know, they know what causes that."

"Haha." Jason stuck his tongue out and rolled his eyes.

It was good to see that parenthood hadn't changed the partners' love for fun.

"When will you know if it's a boy or girl?" Beth's timidness had waned, but she continued to be shy around the whole group.

"Funny you should ask." Mel rested her head on Jason's shoulder. "The doc messed up when he checked the boxes for my latest blood test and ordered an NIPT."

"A what?" Cassidy asked.

"A noninvasive prenatal testing. It's used to check for chromosomal conditions. But it can also tell the gender early on."

"And?" Kyle prodded.

"Everything is normal, not that it would have mattered to us, but it's nice to know." Jason beamed at his wife. "And according to the test, we're having a boy."

Whoops and cheers filled the room.

"I know it's early, but do you have name ideas yet?" Doug loved that his friends were adding to the family again. Thanks to this group and the woman snuggled against him, his life had never been so full.

"We have." Melanie placed her hand on Dennis's shoulder. "Jason and I decided on the name James. And if by surprise it's a girl, then it will be Jamie."

Dennis's jaw dropped, and Doug thought he saw tears fill the man's eyes.

Jason cleared his throat. "You've helped each and every one of us through difficult times. You've covered our shifts without complaint when life happened. You've been our boss and our friend. And sometimes a pain in our backside."

The group laughed at Dennis's playful glare at Jason.

"All that to say, Dennis James Monroe, we'd like to name our son after you, if that's okay."

Charlotte's hand clasped her husband's. It took a moment for his friend and boss to find his voice. "I'm not sure what to say except that I'm honored."

After a few moments of soft conversation, the group fell back into the usual racket when the lot of them got together.

Doug tucked Hope in tight, eased an arm around Beth's shoulder, and pulled her close. He kissed the top of her head. "Having fun?"

She tilted her head and smiled. "I am." She jutted her chin toward Jason and Melanie. "I know you were teasing earlier, and I do need time. But once Miss Hope is old enough, I'd like to add to the baby count."

His heart almost exploded with joy. "I'd love that. As many as you want, whenever you're ready."

"Really?" Her green eyes held his gaze.

"Honey, when it comes to you, I want to make your dreams come true."

Beth rose on her tiptoes and brushed her lips against his. "You and Hope are my dream."

"And you're mine." If he had the power, he'd give his wife the moon. She'd endured a lot in her life, and he had every intention of filling her days with so much love she'd never doubt her worth—ever again.

* * * * *

If you liked this story from Sami A. Abrams,
check out her previous
Love Inspired Suspense books,

Killer Christmas Evidence
Detecting Secrets
Twin Murder Mix-Up
Buried Cold Case Secrets

Available now from Love Inspired Suspense!

Find more great reads at
www.LoveInspired.com.

Dear Reader,

Thank you for reading Doug and Tabitha's story of inner strength and finding the courage to fight against fear. As the saying goes, God will never give you more than you can handle. Well, these two are a prime example of that. So, in hard times, hold on to 1 Corinthians 10:13.

I'm sad to say that this is the final book in the Deputies of Anderson County series. I hope you've loved these characters as much as I do. I know I will miss them. (Maybe, just maybe, you'll see a few of the secondary characters in future stories.)

A special shoutout to my agent, Tamela Hancock Murray, and to my editor, Shana Asaro. You two are the best! I absolutely love working with you. To editor Caroline Timmings for helping me to make this book better. And thank you to my Suspense Squad girls. Knowing there's a group of writers who I can call at any time for writing help or just to laugh is amazing. Thank you, ladies. You're awesome!

Thank you to my law enforcement consultant, Detective James Williams, Sacramento Internet Crimes Against Children, who answers all my crazy questions. By the way, all mistakes are my own or are author privilege, so don't complain to him. Lol!

And thank you to my family for their love and support. Love you bunches, Darren, Matthew, and Melissa!

I'd love to hear from you. Visit my website at samiaabrams.com and sign up for my newsletter to receive exclusive subscriber news and giveaways.

Hugs,
Sami A. Abrams